You and Me

A MISTY RIVER ROMANCE NOVELLA

Becky Wade

I'm grateful to the wonderful women who helped me with this novella! Charlene Patterson, editor extraordinaire. Courtney Walsh, my friend and fellow author, designed this beautiful cover. Katie Ganshert assisted with brainstorming and Dani Pettrey prayed me through. Joy Tiffany, Crissy Loughridge, Amy Watson, and Shelli Littleton graciously served as first readers and encouragers.

Thank you all!

Chapter One

Connor Bryant's biggest crush ever struck when he was in the seventh grade.

Sixteen years had passed, and he was finally on his way to do something about that crush. He zipped his quilted gray jacket as he navigated around the residents and tourists packing Misty River's historic downtown. Light spilled over him from one storefront window after another as he made his way through the dark, cold, crisp December night toward the town square.

When he was a kid, he'd been an ingredient list of things that had helped him go unnoticed. Shy, pale, skinny, red-haired, not very athletic. By the time he'd graduated from elementary, his approach to school had been cemented.

He kept his head down. He was polite. He was quiet. He was kind. He flew under the radar. Which explained why, when he showed up for seventh grade art class at Misty River Middle

School, he slightly acknowledged the kids he knew but didn't register the strangers at all. Shay Seaver was a stranger to him, so it hadn't been crush at first sight.

It was only over time that he began to notice the tomboy girl who wore her light brown hair in a ponytail. She wasn't an over-talker, but she also wasn't afraid to contribute in class. In fact, she didn't appear to be afraid of anything. Almost every other middle schooler, including him, was sixty percent self-conscious. Not her.

She didn't seem to feel the need to impress anyone. Trends in clothing, music, and TV were of no interest to her. She ran cross country, never wore makeup, hated spiders, loved her two good friends, was a huge fan of the Miracle Five, and memorized Broadway show tunes. Shay Seaver knew who she was.

Connor's crush on her developed like a photo in liquid solution—over time.

He reached the end of the block and turned left. The town of Misty River sat in the Blue Ridge mountains of northern Georgia like a toy boat in the swells of the sea. It was Saturday, December fifth, and the annual parade and Christmas tree lighting would occur soon, which explained the crowd and the fact that all the businesses were still open, hosting "open houses," and giving away hot cider, Christmas cookies, fudge, and more.

In a nod to its 1823 founding, the historic district was decorated in an "Old-Fashioned Christmas" theme. Fake fruit and nuts dotted the greenery woven around lampposts and tied with large red-and-white-checked ribbon. Matching wreaths hung on almost every window. More than one truck driver had lived to regret their decision when they'd tried to pass under the white Christmas lights zigzagging back and forth across the cobblestone streets.

It had been at Christmastime all those years ago when his crush on Shay had reached full force. At that point, it became the most overwhelming crush anyone had experienced since the beginning of time. He'd been physically heartsick over her when they were apart. When he was near her, his pounding pulse and his fear of saying the wrong thing meant that he'd spoken to her very little.

Instead of having actual conversations with her, he'd imagined the ways he could become her superhero. Someone would trip her in a cross-country race. She'd twist an ankle. He'd carry her over the finish line, set her down, then punch the guy who'd tripped her. But then he'd remember that she probably only competed against girls and suddenly punching a girl in the face didn't seem very heroic.

He'd imagine that her house was on fire, and he'd rush inside, calling her name. Courageously, he'd guide her from the collapsing building. Her sooty face would look at him with a dawning sense of love. But then he'd remember that she probably wouldn't have been home alone and leaving the rest of her family members inside the burning building didn't seem very romantic.

He'd imagine she was giving a presentation in the auditorium when the kids started to boo her. He'd stand and yell that Shay, and her presentation, were wonderful and perfect and if they couldn't see that, they were all idiots. Shay, grateful tears in her eyes, would draw him up the steps beside the stage, pull him behind the curtain, and hold his hand. But then he'd remember that there were probably administrators behind the curtain, which didn't seem very intimate.

Those were just three of the scenarios he remembered. Eventually, he'd dreamt up hundreds. Not only had none of his scenarios ever happened, but it had turned out that Shay wasn't the type who needed rescuing.

The storefront of Shay's stationery shop, Papery, came into view.

Both he and Shay continued to choose art as their elective all the way through high school. Painting was Connor's passion, calling, dream. Shay had been drawn to calligraphy and graphic design.

Across six years of art class together, he'd gradually gained the ability to speak to her—mostly because she was outgoing and genuine, one of the easiest people to talk to in their entire grade. They grew to be friends. Not close friends. But friends.

He'd carefully watched for even a small signal that she was interested in more than friendship with him. But that signal had never come.

When he'd graduated from high school, his primary feeling had not been excitement. His primary feeling had been grief over losing his connection to Shay. As he'd driven across the country in a packed Suburban so that his mom could move him into the housing at California Institute of the Arts, all his thoughts had been for Shay.

It seemed impossible that a girl who'd never been his girlfriend could break his heart. But his heart *had* broken across that first semester.

To his surprise, plenty of college girls had been eager to raise his spirits. They'd pursued him.

They'd seen him the way he'd wanted Shay to see him. In response, he'd done his best to find happiness in them, in partying, in physical pleasure. He'd gained experience, sure that the next girl or the next would finally remove his feelings for Shay.

Ultimately, his actions hadn't brought him happiness. Just emptiness.

He'd rediscovered his faith and, with it, his center. Graduated. And worked in LA for the next four years.

Through it all, Shay had stubbornly remained in his mind and dreams. He'd returned to Georgia for visits and seen her from time to time—which never failed to send a shaft of electricity through him. They'd talk, and he'd experience euphoria. Sorrow, too, for a few reasons. One, he'd catalog the changes in her and realize how much he'd missed. Two, he'd been painfully aware their time together would end too quickly. Three, she was always dating someone and he wasn't the type of guy who'd tell a woman how he felt about her while she was in a relationship with another man.

He pushed open Papery's door and walked inside. Her shop reminded him of his niece's birthday parties. Creative, festive, full of bright pastels. Pale blue walls and white shelving neatly stocked with products framed the central table she used when she met with clients. At the moment, the whole place was decked out with Christmas items. Little trees. Gifts, ornaments, cards, and more.

He didn't see Shay, which meant she'd probably ducked into her office. Tonight was an important night for her business, so she'd be here somewhere.

Gabe, Shay's one employee, was waiting on a group of four customers. At seven feet tall, Gabe had dressed in a blue shirt, suspenders, trousers, and a cap. Clearly, he'd taken the town up on their invitation to business owners to dress in 1800s style.

"My, you're tall," Connor overheard one of the customers saying to Gabe. "Do you play basketball?"

Gabe's dark brown skin creased as an engaging smile overtook his face. Connor knew people asked Gabe that question constantly, yet Gabe responded with good humor every time.

"Nah," Gabe said. "I tried. Turns out, it takes skill to play basketball." He shrugged. "I don't have any."

Just then Shay sailed from the back room into the retail space, arms full of at least twenty rolls of wrapping paper.

The sight of her impacted his chest like a ball of starlight.

Her face brightened when she spotted him. "Hi, Connor."

"Hi."

"How are you?"

"Really well . . ." *Now that I'm with you.* "Want me to hold some of these for you?"

"Yes, please." She stopped in front of him, and he took more than half the wrapping paper off her hands. One by one, she thrust the rolls into a tall wicker basket. "Can I help you with anything specific?"

"No, I just have a question for you."

"Cool. Let me get the rest of these situated and I'm all yours."

"No hurry."

She usually wore an apron at work, but tonight she'd gone with a costume like Gabe's. Where Gabe's cotton shirt was blue, hers was strawberry red. Her suspenders were white and instead of a hat, she'd tied fabric with holly leaves on it around her neck as a kerchief. She looked adorable.

She took some rolls from him and added them to a display. Then she took the rest to an antique metal bin.

Though she was only five-foot-four, eight inches shorter than Connor, Shay's presence was tall. Energy vibrated from her, and efficiency marked the movements of her small hands. Her frame, which had always held the lean muscles of a runner, now also held the curves of a woman. A few years back, she'd added some strands of honey-gold to the almond-brown of her shoulder-length hair. As an adult, she wore ponytails occasionally and makeup daily.

The thing that had never changed? Her big, bright smile. It had the power to light up rooms.

Time had dissipated the shyness of his boyhood the way sun evaporates a water puddle. He chose his words carefully and he'd never be the most confident man in the room. But these days, people told him they found him approachable and called him things like "mellow" and a "good listener."

He'd changed. Shay had changed. They were twenty-eight years old now.

Yet she was still the one for him.

It might not be fashionable to fall in love for life in middle school, but that's what he'd done. He was past thinking he might get over his feelings for her.

Shay made a sound of irritation and pointed to a long Christmas paper chain that lay on the floor like a dead snake. "This fell again. Would you mind helping me put it back?"

"Not at all." He lifted the chain.

She leaned over the cash register's counter and returned carrying a box of tacks. "It's supposed to swag charmingly across the front of this." She indicated a display case.

He held up the chain and she stood back, head tilted to the side, issuing instructions.

Hers wasn't the kind of beauty that smacked you the first time you saw her. It was the kind that snuck up on you little by little until it was shaking you by the collar and robbing all your air. Her heart-shaped face held a fresh, girl-next-door type of beauty. She had clear skin and pale brown eyes that danced and crinkled.

"Another inch to the left," she suggested.

He complied.

Since he'd moved back to Misty River two years ago, Connor had become a regular at Papery. He custom-ordered all his art supplies through Shay. He could have saved money by ordering them himself but the opportunity to talk with her and the satisfaction he received from supporting her business more than made up the difference.

They also hung out now and then at social gatherings. Up until two months ago, however, she'd been dating a guy named Nate. Nate had seemed even less worthy of her than her past boyfriends, so it had been one of the happiest days of Connor's year when he'd heard that Shay and Nate had broken up.

"That looks perfect, right there." She passed him some tacks and he secured the first swag of the paper chain to the top of the unit. Then he held up the next swag, waiting while she eyeballed it. She nibbled delicately on the edge of her lip, and he swallowed a groan as his attention fixed on her mouth.

"A smidge to the right?" she said. "Yep."

He and Shay were both finally single. They both finally lived in the same town. Right after her relationship with Nate ended, Connor had known he needed to make his move. But for the first several weeks, she'd been in mourning over the end of her romance. He didn't want to rush her, but he couldn't wait too long. She might get back together with Nate. Or she might start dating someone new. If that happened before he said anything, he'd never forgive himself. So he'd come up with a plan.

He tacked up more of the paper chain.

"What question did you have for me?" she asked, continuing to assess her display.

"There's a woman that I really like—"

"Oh?" Her pretty brows lifted, and her expression sharpened on him with curiosity. "Who?"

"I'd rather not say." He'd prepared for this question. "Misty River's small. Everyone knows everyone and I'd feel uncomfortable having to . . . tell you who she is at this point."

"A mystery?" she asked with delight.

"A mystery," he confirmed.

"How about we call her Molly?"

"Why Molly?"

"Because Molly is the name of the American marathoner who won a medal at the last Olympics." To this day, Shay went running every morning except Sunday and followed TV coverage of marathons, Iron Man races, and track and field. "Plus, I don't know anyone named Molly in this town."

"Molly it is."

"What's your question concerning Molly?"

He gestured with his head, asking, *Is this where you want me to tack the end of this paper chain?* without words.

She nodded. The group of customers followed Gabe to the checkout counter.

Connor pushed in the final tack. "I want to bring my A game with Molly." His arms dropped and he slid his hands into the pockets of his jacket.

"I haven't dated much lately, and I think I could use a consultant. I wondered if you'd consider being that . . . for me."

She neared, rattling the box of tacks in a loose fist. "Your dating consultant?"

"Exactly. To whip me into shape."

"In what way?"

"How I look, how I dress, how I go about asking Molly out."

"I don't think you need whipping into shape."

"There's room for improvement," he said honestly.

"Not much."

"But some. This is important to me." The caramel flecks in her eyes made it hard to concentrate enough to organize words. "I want to give myself the best possible chance with her." And, after a lot of thought, he had confidence that this strategy would give him that. The best possible chance. It provided two benefits he needed if he was going to have a shot—more time one-on-one with Shay and insights into what she found attractive.

He was also painfully aware of the potential pitfalls. When he told her *she* was Molly she might say that she felt nothing more than friendship for him. Or she might feel deceived and react with anger. The former was very likely. The latter less so, based on what he knew of her.

Thing was, nothing worth having was without risk.

And Shay was worth all the risk in the world. He was ready to push all of his chips to the center of the table.

"It sounds like Molly's inspired quite a bit of devotion in you," Shay said.

"Yes."

"Lucky girl." She rattled the tacks again. "How come you want me as your consultant?"

Because your opinion on these things is the only one that matters to me. "I think you and Molly are a lot alike. You have similar taste."

"Oh?" She winked at him. "She's sporty, classy, and drop dead gorgeous?"

He chuckled. "Exactly."

"If she's wonderful enough to have inspired your devotion, then she's wonderful enough to like you just the way you are, Connor. I'll tell you the same thing I tell all my other friends and myself. You shouldn't change who you are for someone else."

"I don't want to change who I am." How could he explain this to her? "I want to . . . enhance what's already there so she'll see me. Look what you did with this place." When she'd purchased

Papery it had been dingy and crumbling. "You're good at taking something with potential and making it even more itself than it was before."

She tucked a lock of hair behind one ear. "You simply want me to polish the diamond?"

"Am I"—his brows drew down—"the diamond in this scenario?"

"You're the diamond. And I don't want to change a diamond."

"But you are willing to polish it?"

"Is that what you want? A little polish?"

"Yes. Will you do it?"

For a few seconds, she appeared to weigh the question. "Sure. I'd love to, actually."

"Really?"

"Yes."

"Thank you." He grinned at her, relieved.

"What's your timeline? When do you want to ask Molly out?"

"I want to ask her out before Christmas. I have a few weeks off over the holidays and it would be great to spend time with her while I'm on vacation."

"In that case, should we start now?"

"Now?"

"Almost all the businesses, including this one, are closing in five minutes," she said. "But I know

15

for a fact that Brad over at the barber shop is keeping his doors open until ten."

"You want me to get a haircut?"

"And a shave?"

He'd been so focused on having this conversation with her that he hadn't prepared for anything else. The rest of the evening had been a blank in his mind. "You want me to shave off my beard?" He wasn't typically a spontaneous person.

She beamed at him and his heart contracted. "Are you balking at your dating consultant's very first suggestion?"

"No."

"Mm," she teased, unconvinced.

"I'm not balking," he insisted. "I was surprised, but I'm committed to this process."

"Are you set on keeping Molly's identity anonymous?"

"Yes."

"And you said Molly's taste is like mine?"

"Yes."

"Because . . . I can't speak for all women. I can only advise you on what appeals to me."

"Got it."

"The only way I know to do this is to trust my taste."

"I'm willing to try whatever you recommend."

"Excellent." Then she launched into singing. "'Let us seize the day.' That's from *Newsies*."

"Let us seize the day." Unlike her, he didn't sing the line.

"Wait here while I run and grab my coat?"

"Yeah."

Then, to Gabe, as she hurried past him, "Can you close for me?"

"You bet, boss."

Chapter Two

Well, wasn't this an unexpected pleasure?

Inside her office, Shay swiftly gathered her things. Coat, mittens, hat with the pom-pom on top, purse. One of her patterned socks had dipped too close to her hiking boot, so she pulled the sock back up to her knee and tucked her trousers into its top.

Typically, she enjoyed the Christmas tree lighting celebration. Today, though, memories of prior Christmas tree lightings she'd attended with Nate had haunted every quiet moment. She'd been feeling blue since the moment her alarm had gone off this morning. Everyone else's joviality only made her feel worse by comparison as the workday had dragged on.

But now? Now Connor's surprise proposition had filled her sails with gusts of purpose and excitement. He was a high school art teacher who'd moved back to Misty River to take care of his mom after she'd been diagnosed with ALS. She couldn't think of anyone more deserving of a mini-makeover than Connor.

She found him exactly where she'd left him. Unlike most people their age, he hadn't pulled out his phone in order to fill the forty seconds that she'd been gone.

They ushered outside into the crush of people accumulating for the parade. Shay cut a path forward, moving at twice Connor's factory-set speed. The parade would include the high school marching band, some homespun floats, candy-throwing, numerous pets in Christmas costumes who were available for adoption at Furry Tails, and Santa and Mrs. Claus riding in a motorized sleigh. She'd seen this same parade almost every year of her life. Missing it in order to shine the diamond of Connor? No brainer.

As soon as Brad welcomed them to the barber shop, Shay began communicating her wishes to the older man, using hand gestures to elaborate.

Brad, who was in his mid-forties, listened with amusement. His silver stud earring matched the silver streaks in the hair rising sleekly up and away from his forehead. The earring and hairstyle jibed with his usual hipster clothing. Not so much with the topcoat, breeches, and cravat he wore for tonight's festivities.

Brad looked to Connor. "What do you think about all this?"

"I'm good with it," Connor answered, easygoing as always.

She trusted Brad's work because she'd personally witnessed so many of his transformations. Connor might not have as much motivation to trust Brad but even so, within minutes, Connor had allowed himself to be levered back on the barber shop chair.

No doubt Connor hadn't expected to find himself horizontal, having oil rubbed into his beard and a steam machine aimed at his face, ten minutes after asking if she'd become his dating consultant. She bit back a smile as she remembered his taken-aback response when she'd suggested they do this immediately.

When she set her mind to something, she liked to attack it wholeheartedly. Dilly-dally was not her middle name.

To Connor's credit, he'd risen to the challenge.

Brad wrapped Connor's face in a hot towel. A minute later he removed it and went to work. The straight razor made pleasant scritching sounds.

Shay waited on the edge of her seat, fascinated. She hadn't seen Connor without a beard since they were in high school. Back when they'd met, he'd been a sweet, awkward kid with hair the color of a copper penny. Over the years, his hair had darkened to a deep auburn. His skin was fair, but not milky white. His nose was a straight specimen of masculine perfection. His gray eyes were deep-set and downturned—a fraction lower at their outer edges—which lent him a pensive look that suited him. He was a thinker more than a talker. Observant.

She hadn't decided to axe the beard because it was unattractive. It was about an inch long and well kept. She'd decided to axe it because her intuition was telling her he had a stunning jawline under there. More than that, though, she suspected he hid behind the beard. He'd asked her to enhance what was already there, so that Molly would see him. This seemed like the clear first step.

The beard fell away in strips. When he finished, Brad patted on aftershave that smelled of sage. Then he sat Connor upright and went to work with flashing scissors on Connor's hair, which was thick with a bit of curl.

She was very proud of her first decision as his dating consultant because Connor's smooth cheeks revealed a strong, classic, V-shaped chin.

Brad kept some length on the sides of Connor's

hair, and slightly more length on top. What began to emerge was exactly the hairstyle effect she'd envisioned—tousled and casual, yet neat enough to enhance Connor's gift-from-God bone structure.

Shay and Brad carried on a conversation while Connor regarded himself in the mirror with a bemused expression. He held his body with stillness and patience.

She'd always liked Connor Bryant. In fact, she dared anyone not to like him. He was relaxed and genuine, the sort of person who lowered your blood pressure. Shay's decisive personality gelled with his thoughtful one, making the vibe between them effortless.

They'd spent years in art classes together when they were growing up. During that season, she'd appreciated having him as a friend but hadn't experienced any teen girl bolts of attraction. Then he'd gone away to school and quite a bit of time had passed. When she'd finally seen him again, she'd realized with a startled clang that Connor Bryant had grown into himself. He was more assured. Taller. Mature. Handsome.

In the years since, their interactions had—for her, anyway—been undergirded with a subtle buzz of possibility. However, she'd given that possibility no room to grow. She'd been with Nate for years.

And now, Connor was into Molly.

Brad stepped back, signaling that his work was done.

Shay met Connor's eyes in the mirror. "What do you think?" she asked.

"I like it."

"You're so good-looking!"

"Nah. Brad's an excellent barber."

Humble Connor clearly did not grasp the magnitude of his appeal. She waved an arm from his head to his toes. "You're an extraordinarily good-looking man. Isn't he, Brad?"

"Extraordinarily," Brad answered wryly.

When Connor didn't reply, she gave him a belligerent expression that said, *Speak!*

"Thank you," he said. And then, "How much do I owe you?" to Brad.

Once the bill and tip had been paid, they made their way to the giant fir tree erected in the center of the town square. Shay noticed with smug satisfaction that numerous women shot Connor double-takes or surreptitious glances.

The parade now complete, The Vine Church choir sang *O Christmas Tree* from a small stage. Spectators formed a dense ring around the tree. She and Connor found a vantage point behind a family with enough kids to fill a minivan.

"You mentioned earlier that you haven't dated a lot lately," she said. In fact, now that she thought about it, she couldn't recall him having a girlfriend at all since his return to Misty River. "Any particular reason?"

"My heart wasn't in it."

"Why?"

"I guess because I've liked Molly for a while now. Everyone else seems like a runner-up."

Earlier, Shay had called Molly a lucky girl. She'd meant it. Connor would make an excellent boyfriend. "I'm feeling more and more invested in the task of preparing you to date Molly. What should we tackle next?"

"My wardrobe?"

"Yes! I could meet you Wednesday afternoon."

"Done."

The mayor came on stage. After making a few remarks, she began the countdown to the lighting of the tree. "Ten, nine . . ." The voices of the crowd joined in. "Five, four." Louder. "One!"

Thousands of lights flashed on, illuminating the tree. Icicle lights. Tiny red lights. White twinkle lights. The crystal star on top glinted. Red-and-white-checked ribbon accented some of the boughs. Others held old-fashioned wooden ornaments or clusters of the same fruit-and-nuts combo that decorated the downtown greenery.

The crowd released a collective, "Ahhhh," of wonder. The high school band played "Jingle Bells."

"Shay?"

She turned her chin to him in answer and discovered that he was already looking at her. Light from the tree bathed the clean angles and contours of his face.

"Thank you very much for helping me with this."

He'd single-handedly turned what had been a bummer of a day, thanks to Nate the Disappointment, into a satisfying evening. "Trust me when I say that helping you really has been and will continue to be my pleasure."

• • •

"I don't let myself eat lasagna Monday through Saturday," Connor's mom said to him the following day. "But it's Sunday, praise the Lord. I allow myself lasagna on Sundays."

Accustomed to her food issues, Connor nodded as he cracked open the oven to check the cooking progress on the lasagna he'd purchased for their dinner. Almost done.

"I can't wait." She began unloading the dishwasher. "All that ricotta. The spicy meat. The curvy edges of the noodles." She groaned happily.

The winter sun set early, so the kitchen's windows framed dark views of their neighborhood. It was plenty bright inside, though. In addition to the recessed lighting, his mom had lit a lamp on the counter and a battery-powered one on the table.

He assisted with the dishes as she continued to sing lasagna's praises.

For reasons he didn't understand, she'd chosen to live in a tug-of-war between her deep affection for food and her desire not to gain weight. She was not a petite person, but who cared? She was beautiful as she was. Tall and striking, with a knack for dressing in layers of clothing. She wore her graying strawberry-blond hair in a short style that suited her kind face.

She looked great at the age of sixty and he'd have liked for her to make peace with food so that she could enjoy it for as long as possible before ALS affected her ability to eat and swallow. But, so far, the tug-of-war showed no signs of stopping.

"I'm not planning to eat more than eight ounces of lasagna," she was saying. "I'll whip up a side salad and fill up on that."

Mom had been the rock of his childhood after Dad left the family when Connor was seven. Penny

Bryant was dependable, supportive, and unselfish, which was why the day he'd learned she had Lou Gehrig's disease had been the worst of his life. He'd known just enough about the condition to react with horror. The research he'd done following their phone conversation had deepened his dread. ALS was a heartbreaking, dehumanizing way to die.

How, he'd wondered, could this be his mother's fate? It seemed incredibly unfair that someone so good should be handed such a brutal sentence.

He'd given his landlord and the administrators at his school in LA notice, telling them he'd leave as soon as the fall semester ended. Once he'd fulfilled that commitment, he'd rented a U-Haul truck, packed it with his belongings, and driven across the country as if zombies were chasing him.

When he'd arrived at his childhood home after three marathon days behind the wheel, the house had glowed despite the late hour. Mom had waited up for him, just like in the old days when he'd gone over to his buddy Andrew's house and stayed up till midnight playing video games.

She'd met him halfway between the U-Haul and the front door and wrapped him in a hug. She loved all three of her children fiercely, but he secretly suspected he was her favorite. The two of them were the most alike in their family. Even and dependable.

He'd pulled back and looked at her. "Mom," he said, throat tight.

In the way of mothers, she seemed to understand all of his despair and fear. And in the way of mothers, she acted quickly to comfort him, even though he wasn't the one with the crushing diagnosis.

She gripped his shoulder, her gray eyes steady. She looked tired, yes, but not racked with fear. "This isn't what I would've chosen, but I can't complain, either. I've had a wonderful life. A life I love. There's been heartache"—he knew she was mostly referring to his dad—"but I have you three and so I count myself to be one of the most fortunate women in the world."

Emotions heaving, he'd said nothing.

"I intend to keep on living to the fullest," she continued, "for as long as I can. God has brought me this far and I trust Him to bring me the rest of the way. I'm going to take it one day at a time. And that's what I want you to do, too. I want you to live to the fullest. Trust God. And take it one day at a time."

He stood tall and unwavering, strong for her, though tears filmed his vision.

"We're going to get through this," she promised. "It's going to be all right."

He saw then that she viewed the remainder of her life as her crucial final act of mothering. She was determined to shepherd her children through her death in a way that enabled them to emerge as healthy and whole as possible.

"I'm only sorry you felt you had to give up your life in California," she said.

"I'm not sorry." She needed someone to move in and take care of her. His older sister was married with three young kids. His younger sister lived out of state and was married to her job as the CFO of a start-up. But even if his sisters' circumstances had been different, no one would have doubted, least of all him, that he was the one to do this job.

His sisters were loud, bossy, dramatic. He was none of those things. He had the type of personality that could weather hard conversations with doctors, endless appointments, and the administration of medicines.

He wanted to be her rock, as she had been his.

"There's nowhere else I'd rather be than here," he'd told her.

All his life, he'd witnessed her courage and grace. But never more than in the two years that had followed his homecoming.

Sometimes, ALS took people with gut-wrenching speed. Sometimes, it moved more slowly. His family had expected the worst at the outset, but so far, the progression of the disease had been gradual. God had gifted his mother with additional time.

She wore leg braces and walked with a cane. She took oral medicine and rounds of IV medicine. She dealt with physical therapy and testing.

She'd been a librarian at the city library her entire career. When her boss learned of her condition, he'd invited Mom to work by the hour—as little or as much as she desired. Mom still went to the library for a portion of each weekday.

She took the same approach to housework. He'd repeatedly told her that she didn't have to do anything around the house. She'd repeatedly shown him that helping out soothed her. It made her feel she was contributing and gave her a connection to the rhythms she'd been practicing for years.

Every time he'd had a vacation from work, they'd traveled. Sometimes with a sister or two and the grandkids. Mom had chosen the destinations and chosen well. They'd been to Aspen in winter. Maine and Montana in summer. Lake Tahoe and

Santa Fe for spring break.

Except when one of his noisy sisters was on the phone or in the house, he and Mom lived peacefully. They understood each other. She accepted his help. He respected her independence.

He no longer felt the sharp edge of anxiety that had initially consumed him. But at times, the heaviness of her prognosis wore him down. He struggled with loneliness, which was strange because he was surrounded by kids and fellow teachers at work and spent time with Mom after work. Turned out that serving as the caregiver for someone deteriorating from ALS brought with it a unique kind of loneliness that wasn't easy to explain.

She eased into a chair as he finished putting away the last of the dishes. He started setting the table.

"Have you heard any updates on the live nativity?" she asked. For the past fifteen years, she'd organized Misty River's live nativity. It ranked just below food and above travel on her list of passions. She still attended most of the nativity committee meetings, though volunteers had lifted almost all the responsibilities from her shoulders.

"I meant to tell you earlier and forgot." He'd spent the last several hours in his studio, lost in

31

painting and thoughts of Shay. "In addition to the donkey and sheep, Sam Turner told me that he's confirmed an alpaca and a miniature cow."

Her mouth dropped open and a hand pressed to her heart. "An alpaca! A miniature cow!"

Connor hadn't known there was such a thing as miniature cows. And he definitely didn't think that there'd been alpacas in Bethlehem. But Sam had agreed months ago to host the nativity at Sugar Maple Farm, his historic property on national park land. Connor was so grateful to the guy that he wasn't about to question either animal.

"We're going to have the best nativity ever this year," Mom said.

"The very best." Her primary goal this month was to pull off a meaningful live nativity. Since that was her goal, it had become Connor's.

"You know who I'm going to contact, to see if she'd be interested in a character role?" she asked.

"Who?"

"Shay Seaver."

He paused with silverware in his hands to cut a look in her direction. Her profile was a mask of innocence as she considered her perfect burgundy nail polish.

"Oh?" He set the silverware on napkins. As much as he liked his mom, he did not want her butting into his love life.

"I think she'd be fabulous. There's something so . . . bright and endearing about her."

"Mm," he said noncommittally. Inwardly, though, he agreed. In a rush, he remembered how she'd looked last night at the Christmas tree lighting. The sweep of her thick eyelashes. The small earrings sparkling in her ears. The fabric tied around her delicate throat.

Longing chased the memory, deep and true.

Chapter Three

Shay had purposely proposed that she meet Connor at his house on Wednesday afternoon before they went shopping for clothes. She wanted to A) check on his mother, the woman she credited with fostering her love of reading and B) see where Connor lived and painted.

She'd told herself that B was important because it would give her insight that would help her gauge Connor's style of fashion. But really. In the days since he'd asked her to serve as his dating consultant, her curiosity about him had been growing. She didn't know Connor as well as she should, after their long acquaintance. Like most unselfish men, he didn't talk about himself often. Seeing where he lived would provide detail.

She made her way up the walkway to the Bryants' craftsman bungalow. The temperature hovered in the mid-fifties and rain fell steadily onto her umbrella from low, white clouds. Sodden leaves carpeted the earth, leaving the bare branches of the trees shiny and dark with water. Breathing in the damp cool, she was glad she'd chosen black camo leggings, a gray exercise top, and a pale pink work-out jacket.

The homes in this section of town were all over a century old and full of character. The bungalow's porch spanned the width of the house. The exterior brick had been painted a dark brownish gray, the trim white.

Mrs. Bryant answered the door, her face creasing with pleasure at the sight of Shay. They hugged and exchanged greetings.

It had been several months since Shay's path had crossed with Mrs. Bryant's. She'd worried about the state she'd find her in today, so it was reassuring to see her looking so much like herself. She wasn't moving as easily as she once had. But there was still color in her cheeks and strength in her limbs.

"I love your house," Shay said honestly.

"Thank you!"

Antiques were interspersed with newer rugs, pillows, upholstered ottomans, soft chairs. Hardwood floors stretched to walls painted creamy white. The overall effect was cozy and welcoming.

"This is the house Connor's dad and I bought

soon after we were married," Mrs. Bryant said. "Three bedrooms, two bathrooms, a million memories. Best investment ever. Come." She beckoned. "Let me show you around."

Shay admired the living room, dining room, and kitchen before they reached the hallway, where she spotted Connor coming in from the back door.

His gait hitched when he saw her. A slow, lop-sided smile moved across his face. He wore his usual uniform of a patterned button-down shirt, untucked, over jeans. There'd never been anything wrong with his wardrobe, per se. It was just so vanilla that it didn't show him off to his best advantage.

"Hi," he said. "You're early."

"Yep. Your mom's giving me a tour."

Mrs. Bryant opened a door, revealing her master bedroom. Then she showed Shay the room her girls had shared. "They had bunkbeds once, but a double bed with trundles on either side makes more sense now, when they come to stay."

The hall bath gleamed. "Has this been newly renovated?" Shay asked.

"Yes. When Connor moved back a few years ago he volunteered to update this bathroom and his bedroom."

"I worried she might not want to change any-thing," Connor said.

"He worried for nothing. I've always loved house projects." Connor's mom moved along to his room.

Here, Shay brazenly stepped inside.

"We boxed up the keepsakes," Mrs. Bryant said, "and gave the rest to charity. We painted, then he furnished it with things he'd brought back from LA."

He'd chosen a very dark, moody green for the walls. She'd have been terrified to try this shade, but it absolutely worked. It made her feel as if she was inside a luxurious malachite box. Plus, the color complemented the wood in the room and the white and gray in the bedding. Modern art made the room feel sophisticated—a bit like a gallery. "Where did you come by the art?"

"Those are all originals I purchased when I lived in California. I know several of the artists."

Suddenly, her small-town life and the fact that she'd attended college just four hours away, in Statesboro, made her experiences seem provincial. "These pieces are fabulous."

"I made brownies," Mrs. Bryant said. "They're fresh out of the oven." They made their way to the kitchen. "I typically don't eat much dessert, except for on Wednesday evenings. I weigh myself on Wednesday mornings. So, immediately after that, I splurge."

"I never pass up a brownie," Shay said.

Mrs. Bryant served brownies, then sat at the kitchen table to enjoy her portion while Connor and Shay stood, eating their brownies off small paper plates.

"I was so pleased when Connor told me you were coming by today," Mrs. Bryant told her. "I've been wanting to ask if you'd prayerfully consider playing a role in the live nativity."

"Oh?" She knew just enough about the nativity to know Mrs. Bryant had long been in charge.

"I think you'd make a wonderful angel."

Shay laughed. "*What?*"

"An angel. You have such a wholesome look about you. You're beautiful as can be."

"I am?"

"You are! I've seen the site and plan to place the angels slightly to the side and uphill from the manger scene. We'll have you spotlighted in such a way that you'll appear to glow."

"I'll glow?"

"It will just require one night of work," Mrs. Bryant continued. "Three and a half hours, on December twenty-third."

Shay was not an actress. At all. Nor did she consider herself to be particularly angelic. Turned out that she was angelic enough, however, not to want to disappoint this particular woman. Mrs. Bryant was battling ALS. Mrs. Bryant had once read *Charlotte's Web* aloud to Shay while Shay and other kids sat on the alphabet rug in the Kids' Corner at the library, their faces upturned, riveted by the story. "I'll gladly help out in any way you'd like," Shay said.

"Including as an angel?"

"Yes, ma'am."

"Call me Penny."

"Yes, Penny."

"Wonderful! I'm delighted. Thank you." She helped herself to more brownie. "I'll just have one more smidge of this. Seeing as how it's Wednesday."

"Ready to head out?" Connor asked her.

"I'd like to see your studio before we go shopping, if you don't mind."

"I don't mind at all." They tossed their plates in the trash and said their good-byes to Penny.

Still tasting chocolate, she followed Connor to the structure built in their spacious side yard. "The bones of this have been here for a while, right?" She paused outside, surveying it.

"Yeah. Back when we were kids, Mom came across a book at the library on greenhouse gardening. She got all excited about it and built this. For a couple of years, she remained gung ho. But then she lost steam and decided she wasn't called to become a greenhouse gardener after all. At that point, I was already into art, so she let me clean it out and move some easels in. I painted here in high school."

"Was it hot and steamy inside?"

"It was too hot most of the time and too cold some of the time. Even so, I painted in here quite a bit. I was desperate for privacy from my sisters."

"How many square feet is it?"

"Five hundred."

He held open the door.

She entered, wonder filtering over her. The exterior had appeared impressive, but you had to enter to fully appreciate it. "Did you upgrade this at the same time as your bedroom and bathroom?"

"Yeah."

He'd bricked the floor and replaced three of the walls with wood. The remaining greenhouse frame supported windows—one whole wall of them as well as a peaked ceiling of them. She could both feel and hear the whir of central heat. "It's magnificent."

"Thanks. In good weather, I open some of the ceiling panels and these doors." Demonstrating, he pushed the double glass doors set in the wall of windows open partway. A gust blew in, stirring through her hair. He shut them with a click.

"I'm glad I'm here on a rainy day," she said. "The droplets are making amazing moving patterns."

"I love this space more than any studio I've worked in before because it's so in tune with the weather, the light, nature. From my stool, I can look up and see the mood of the mountains. It's beautiful at sunset. When storms are rolling in. When there's mist and clouds."

"I'm jealous. This is a dream studio."

His materials sat on shelves. Tarps stretched below easels holding four different pieces of art in various stages of completion. He was still pursuing the genre that had always interested him—contemporary abstract art. However, at a glance, she could tell that he'd matured greatly in the years since she'd last seen his work.

She approached the wooden apparatus waiting on the table. "Is this a silk screen?"

"Yes. In college, I settled into a mixed media approach. I use a combination of painting and silk-screen work. I add texture to the piece with several different tools as I go." He stuck his fingers into the front pockets of his jeans.

"So, is creating art your calling and teaching art the thing that pays the bills?"

"The first few years after college, I tried to support myself with my art alone. I didn't have a following yet. Like most artists, I couldn't make a living at it. So, I took classes and eventually got my teaching certificate. It started out as a way to pay the bills, but it turned out the balance of work and art suited me more than I expected."

"How so?"

"Teaching forced me past my tendency to live like a hermit. My art benefitted when I started getting out in the world. I benefitted from getting to know the kids and my coworkers."

Word on the street was that he was an excellent teacher. Patient, a man who genuinely liked people. She could see how he'd gain satisfaction from sharing his knowledge and encouraging teenagers.

"We were lucky to have Mrs. Kirby as our teacher," she said. Mrs. Kirby had been grandmotherly and enthusiastic. She'd believed so much in her students that she'd inspired them to believe in themselves.

"Very lucky," he agreed. "She was a phenomenal teacher."

"And now you're that same source of inspiration for a whole new generation of students." No doubt, a swath of his female students were taking art specifically so they could swoon over Mr. Bryant.

"I hope to be a source of inspiration. Though I can't fill Mrs. Kirby's shoes." Then, dryly, "Especially not the high-heeled pairs."

On a sound of amusement, Shay moved to the most finished-looking piece of art—a stunning work on a large canvas easily five feet by four feet. Blue, beige, white, and gray, the piece gave testament to the long hours of work he'd invested. It was subtle and calming, yet powerful. An intriguing interplay of texture and color. She considered herself to have a decent eye for art and this was exactly the kind of painting she'd have loved to own.

The longer she pondered it, the more her appreciation grew. "Connor?"

"Yes?" he asked, uncertain. She understood the uncertainty. It always made her feel vulnerable when she allowed others to view her card and stationery designs in progress.

"I think this is brilliant." She glanced at him.

His expression said, *You do?*

"Are you ready for me to go poetic on you?" she asked.

"I'm an artist. You can go poetic on me anytime."

She motioned to it. "It reminds me of thunderclouds departing over water at low light."

"Thank you." His gray eyes communicated gratitude.

"You're welcome." Their gazes held. Time pulled like sweet caramel.

Who is Molly? Who was the person who was going to score this gem of a man?

If Molly was near Connor's age and living in Misty River—Wait. She shouldn't assume this person lived in Misty River. Maybe she didn't. But if she did, chances were good that Shay knew her. Indeed, that was probably why Connor had declined to reveal Molly's identity.

She really hoped Molly wasn't Finley Sutherland from Furry Tails Animal Rescue Center. Finley was gorgeous and a living saint when it came to animals. When compared to Finley, Shay didn't stand a chance.

"Can I use Thunderclouds Departing Over Water at Low Light as the painting's title?" he asked.

"Certainly."

"In fact, I don't like titling. So, before you go, can you title the rest of these?" His lips curved sheepishly.

"Is Thunderclouds Departing Over Water at Low Light complete?"

"Nearly."

"When the next one gets to this same stage of completion, let me know. I'll swing back by to spread more of my titling magic."

"Deal."

"Where do you sell these?"

"At a gallery in LA and also the Cameron Gallery here in Misty River."

"Let's stop by the Cameron Gallery before we hit the clothing store so I can shower you with more compliments."

"What if shopping for new clothes takes a lot of time? I wouldn't want to monopolize your whole evening."

"I don't think it'll take a lot of time. But if it does, great. You're my best shot at high-quality entertainment today."

"Nobody's ever called me high-quality entertainment. Not sure I'll measure up."

Connor was a unicorn—both gorgeous *and* modest.

His clean-shaven face was disarming in a way

his bearded face hadn't been. With his thick, faintly disheveled hair and lean, fit frame he looked like what he wasn't—a wealthy New Englander who'd casually accepted the gifts of wealth and looks that had dropped in his lap.

"It's not every day that handsome, talented men ask me to provide my advice," she said. "I happen to enjoy providing advice. Especially to handsome, talented men. So, c'mon." She turned toward the studio door. "This is going to be fun."

• • •

"In the name of full disclosure," Shay said to him from outside his dressing room an hour later, "I'm realizing that this might be the first time I've been inside a clothing store that's just for men. That said, I don't want you to revoke my consultant credential. I still think I can do a really good job at this."

"Nothing would motivate me to revoke your credential." *Literally nothing, seeing as how this whole enterprise is about you.* He finished tucking in the shirt she'd picked and confronted his reflection.

He didn't spend a lot of time thinking about his appearance. In college, he and his friends had participated in a "No-shave November" challenge.

At the end of that month, he'd liked the beard he'd started, so he'd kept it. Then unintentionally left it on his face for eight years.

When it came to clothes, he was visual enough to notice what was current. The few times a year he bought new items, he had the ability to recognize what suited his body and personality. However, he could admit that he'd been stuck in a rut for a while. Maybe to his detriment, because he reached for plain, unremarkable garments every time.

He'd given Shay control over these decisions because he was easy-going about them. He'd never considered himself to be someone who cared very much about his clothes or his hair.

Shay had brought him to Brad the barber. And trusting her and Brad had been a good call because the result had been a clear improvement.

But this outfit? Not an improvement. He looked lame. And he was suddenly realizing that he apparently did care about clothes. Because he didn't want to walk around in things that made him feel like a clown.

She'd put him in a bright patterned shirt and pants that were too skinny. Would letting Shay see him in this hurt his chances with her?

No turning back now. She was waiting for him

to show this outfit to her.

He opened the dressing room door.

She winced from her position on the small bench facing the two dressing rooms. The one next to his was empty.

"I'm not really into stretchy pants," he said.

"Noted. I went for an artsy vibe but now I see the error of my ways. You're artistic, but you're not flashy or super trendy." She stood. "Simple, tailored pieces will flatter you better. Then again, we don't want them to be dull. Hmm. I'll be right back!"

He remained where he was. From here, he could see a slice of the retail area. One customer was working his way through sweaters, one was trying on shoes.

"Ron? Is your name Ron?" she asked an employee. "Hi, I'm Shay. I could use your expertise." She'd never met a stranger.

Connor watched, entertained, as she flashed back and forth across the shop's square footage with Ron trailing her. It always felt like he'd received a surprise gift when he had the chance to study her without her knowing.

Back in the studio, her praise of his art had meant more to him than the most glowing review from an art critic could have. Then, in a one-two punch, she'd met his eyes for a long moment, which had sent desire humming through his bloodstream.

"He's understated but creative," Shay informed Ron. "I don't want him to blend into the background, but he won't want anything showy."

If Shay was a Spice Girl, she'd be Sporty Spice. On her, athletic wear looked business chic. It tagged her as a person who went running in the mornings and checked ten things off her to-do list before breakfast.

She returned, pressing more garments into his hands. "Two more outfits."

He closed himself inside the dressing room. "What are your plans this Christmas?"

"The usual. I'll be tugged like a dog toy between my parents. I never get the feeling that either of them really wants the toy. They just don't want the other one to have it."

He unbuttoned the bright shirt and returned it to its hanger. "Explain." He knew the basics of her history thanks to the town grapevine, but they'd never been close enough for her to share the painful aspects of her childhood with him. He wanted to hear about it in her own words.

"When I was in third grade and my brother, Reece, was in fifth, my mom caught my dad having an affair with Cindy Richter. You might know her, she's the manager at Whiskey's."

"I don't know her."

"Anyway, Mom's discovery of the affair caused a very dramatic scene. I'll never forget all the screaming and weeping and throwing of breakable things. It didn't end that night. It continued for days. Terrible confrontations. Both of them hurting each other." She sighed.

He wanted to wring her parents' necks for putting her through that. "What happened afterward?"

"I don't want to bore you."

"You're not. What happened?"

"They divorced and my dad married Cindy, who also had one boy and one girl. Cindy's kids are just offset by a year from Reece and me and it became a competition in my mom's mind. Mom and her two kids versus Cindy and Cindy's two kids. It was and is exhausting."

In his mind there was no competition. No one he'd ever met had compared to Shay. "Did your mom remarry?"

"She married the first man who came along and ended up getting lucky. He's very long-suffering."

"Did he have kids?"

"No. His first marriage didn't produce any children and he and my mom weren't interested in having more together, which I view as a blessing. It was messy enough as it was. It still is messy. Every holiday is a minefield of decisions."

"How so?"

"Dad only had custody of us every other weekend growing up, so Mom feels like she deserves first dibs on our time. But if it were up to her, we'd never see Dad on a holiday again."

"I'm sorry." And he was.

"My brother is the bright spot of my family. He and I have a great relationship."

"Do you see him often?"

"'Tomorrow, tomorrow, I love ya tomorrow.'" She sang the famous line from *Annie*.

"I don't know anything about music, but I think you have great pitch."

"I'm seeing my brother tomorrow, but I don't see him as often as I'd like. He lives in Dahlonega now with his new wife."

Connor opened the dressing room door again. This outfit he approved of. She'd picked jeans and a rust-colored crewneck sweater under a twill shirt, unbuttoned.

Her expression was like the sun coming out from behind a cloud. She'd crossed her legs and the pink tennis shoe hovering in the air bobbed. "We're definitely getting warmer! That rust color looks great with your hair. Is this comfortable? In your price range? Do you hate it?"

"Yes. Yes. No."

"Try on the next outfit, please. I have a good feeling about it."

He closed himself into the dressing room, shouldered out of the shirt, and stripped the sweater off over his head.

"What about you?" she asked. "Your parents also divorced when you were pretty young, right?"

"Right. I was around the same age that you were when it happened. In the case of my parents, my dad was from England, here on a work visa. My mom fell for his charm and his accent, which didn't prove to be the best basis for marriage."

"Charm is deceptive."

"And beauty is fleeting," he finished the famous verse.

"Did your dad also have an affair?" she asked.

"Not that I know of. He started going back to the UK more and more often for longer periods of time. Eventually, he decided to move back without us. His feelings for my mom had dried up. He didn't want to be married anymore and he was happy parenting us from the other side of the

Atlantic Ocean."

"So he didn't stay in close contact?"

"Not really, no. But by the time the divorce was final, we weren't used to close contact with him, anyway. He came to visit when he felt like it. He called on special occasions and sent gifts on our birthdays. He paid child support. The three of us are his only kids, but he's had several wives. His fourth marriage just collapsed. I don't think he's a bad person, necessarily. He's just not an extremely good one, either."

"Essentially, your mom raised the three of you single-handedly."

"Yes. At holidays, my sisters and I don't get tugged like a dog toy between our parents." He pushed open the door. He wore narrow navy pants and a pale blue button-down. On top of that, a nubby, gray cardigan. On top of that, a relaxed light brown blazer.

Her vision took a slow sweep of him before landing on his eyes. "Can you try buttoning the middle two buttons on the cardigan?"

He did so, then pushed back the sides of the blazer when he slid his hands into his pockets.

A sparkling grin overtook her mouth. "This is it! It reads artist in residence . . . but not in a stuffy way. In a sexy way. It's classic but it has a modern edge." She approached and smoothed down one of the blazer's lapels. That brought her so close he could smell the pear scent of her perfume. He stilled.

And for a moment she did, too.

Their profiles were so close. His heart began to pound—

Blinking, she stepped abruptly back. "Do you love this ensemble? If you don't, I'm going to have to debate you on this one until you do."

"I love it. In part, because I've never been interested in debate."

She rushed toward the center of the shop and returned with Ron.

"Good choices," the older man said admiringly when he came to stand in front of Connor.

"Can you check to make sure everything is fitting him the best way possible?" Shay asked Ron. "I don't know anything about men's sizing."

"Sure."

"Once you figure that out, I'd be extremely grateful if you could help me locate more outfits that have this exact same vibe."

"Absolutely."

Connor looked after his mom. It felt strange

and irresistible to have Shay look after him, even if just for a few minutes.

"Molly won't stand a chance," she told him.

"I hope not."

Chapter Four

Shay's desk in her childhood bedroom would've been the envy of Office Depot.

Around the time her parents' marriage had detonated, she'd quit asking for things as childish as toys for birthday and Christmas gifts. Instead, she'd requested pens in every color, adorable little journals, personalized note cards, notepads, girly scissors, staplers, and dry erase boards. It had seemed to her that if she could fill the air with Broadway tunes and keep her desk cute and organized, then she could maintain some control over her fracturing life.

She'd ended up losing her father's presence in their home and her parents' goodwill toward one another. But she'd never lost her love of stationery.

Mrs. Kirby, her art teacher, had noticed this about Shay. One day when Shay was in eleventh grade, she'd asked, *Have you ever considered a career in stationery design? You could manage your own shop and sell your designs, among other things. It seems to me that's the intersection of your talents and interests.*

Over the weeks that followed, Mrs. Kirby passed her article after article about women who'd built successful stationery lines or successful stationery shops. For the first time, looking at those articles, Shay had seen her future unfold.

The decisions she'd made afterward had been in pursuit of her new dream. She'd selected her college and major accordingly. Her freshman year, she'd begun selling her creations on Etsy. All profit went into a fund for her future business. Same with the profit from the first job she took after graduation, with a graphic design firm. Same with the money she saved by renting the matchbox apartment where she still lived.

Three years after college graduation, she'd saved enough (when combined with capital investments from both parents and a small-business loan) to open Papery.

Three more years had come and gone, and revenue had climbed steadily—almost all of which she folded back into the business. Her designs had taken over more and more of Papery's retail space. She'd funneled her Etsy clients to Papery's website, which enjoyed fantastic traffic. Six months ago, she'd struck up a collaboration with Chic, a chain of women's clothing stores across the South that also stocked items like stationery, bath products, and candles. Her business had grown so much that she'd hit two milestones recently. She'd paid her parents back and hired an employee.

Gabe had finished college a year ago and come to work for her three months later. He'd received a business degree because he'd been undecided about his major and business had seemed like the most sensible choice. It had only taken him a day and a half of working for a stockbroker to realize that he did not want to work for a stockbroker or, indeed, at any kind of business-sector job for the rest of his life. He'd accepted the job at Papery in order to buy himself time to figure out his life plan. So far, he'd explored the ideas of culinary school, employment on cruise ships, and the field of social work.

Affable and trustworthy, Gabe was the ideal employee. She spent more time with him than anyone in her life because of their overlapping work hours. Thus, he'd quickly climbed into her inner circle alongside her brother and Ash and Danielle, the two friends she'd had since elementary school.

On this Thursday afternoon they were alone in

the shop. Aware that their solitude wouldn't last long, they were taking this opportunity to open the newest box of their advent calendar.

The calendar looked like a wooden house, tall and narrow, filled with two-inch square drawers. At the end of November, he'd packed the even days with tiny gifts for her and she'd packed the odd days with tiny gifts for him. At the moment, he stood behind the checkout counter, and she stood on its other side, the calendar between them displayed next to a charming arrangement of boxed Christmas cards.

She slid open the drawer marked "10" to reveal a pink translucent eraser wrapped in cellophane. According to the label, it smelled like peonies. The same measure of delight that would've swept through her at age eight, swept through her at twenty-eight. "A new eraser that smells like peonies!" He knew she had a weakness for both the look and scent of fresh peonies. "You combined two things I love," she said, holding the eraser aloft, "further proving that you're annoyingly good at gift giving."

He winked. "I know."

"I actually love it when I make a mistake with a mechanical pencil because it's so satisfying to smooth it away with an eraser like this one."

"Go wild, boss."

"I intend to. Thank you." She tucked the eraser into the large front pocket of the apron she wore when on the job. Her apron and Gabe's had been hand-made of sturdy beige fabric with *Papery* written across the front in white calligraphy.

She checked her smart watch.

"You've been glancing at your watch a lot this week," Gabe said. "More than usual. Is something going on?"

"Nope. I was just wondering which class Connor's teaching right now. He was telling me about his different classes yesterday. The catatonic group. The loud-talking group. The I-couldn't-care-less-about-art group. And so on."

"You like Connor, don't you?"

"Why do you say that?"

"When you talk about him, you get a . . . dreamy type of expression on your face."

"A dreamy type of expression?"

"Don't look so surprised. You and I both know that you're starting to get into him."

"I . . ." Did she know that? She supposed she did, but she'd been skirting around it in her thoughts.

"Spill." There was nothing Gabe enjoyed more than receiving the inside scoop on the relationships of his friends and family. He prided himself on remaining in the know.

"He's an awesome guy," she stated. "There's never been any doubt of that. He's always been an awesome guy."

"But you didn't have romantic feelings for him until now?"

"I never gave myself permission to have romantic feelings. Then, yesterday, there was this moment when he came out of the dressing room wearing a blazer. It parted to the sides when he stuck his hands in his pockets and—*boom*."

"Boom?"

"I felt this incredible bolt of magnetism, which kind of pinned me to the spot while I attempted to breathe and talk over it."

"The blazer did you in."

"The blazer did me in," she agreed.

"You realized that the awesome guy isn't *just* an awesome guy. You suddenly saw him as boyfriend material."

"In a word . . . yes. It's disorienting when the friendship feelings you've had for ages suddenly morph into a bit of a crush."

"It's best to fall in love with a friend."

"And you make this pronouncement based on your twenty-three years of life experience?"

"I do. I'd be thrilled if you'd date a guy as good as Connor."

She leaned against the counter, sweeping away invisible dust with her fingers.

"Your dad was good in some ways, but deceitful in others," he noted.

She rolled that around. She'd trusted Gabe with her family history, and he'd trusted her with his. "Nicolas, my first long-term boyfriend, was good. It's just that we went to different colleges."

"The common and tragic end of most high school romances."

"My second long-term boyfriend was also good, just more in love with his fraternity than me. Eric was good, but a workaholic who wasn't ready for commitment. Nate was mostly good, but he got complacent."

"Nate took you for granted, which was irritating to watch. Wouldn't it be nice to date someone who's just good, without fine print? Not good *but* a workaholic? Or good *but* complacent?"

"I can't expect perfection! I'm not perfect."

"I think that you and Connor are at similar levels of perfection. If you were houses for sale, you'd be listed at the same price."

She snickered.

"I say go for it and don't waste time." Gabe

put the "10" drawer back in the calendar. "Otherwise someone else is going to take him off the market."

"You're forgetting one hugely important obstacle—" *Oh my word!* Her senses jolted as if she'd stuck a paper clip into an electrical socket. "I think Luke Dempsey just walked past the shop," she hissed.

The two of them sprinted to the front window. All she could see now was the man's retreating back.

She cupped her hands around her eyes and pressed them to the glass, not caring that she'd have to clean the glass later. "We need to go see if that's him."

"He'll notice if someone seven feet tall follows him. You go after him, fast, and text me if he goes into a store. Then I'll pretend to browse there, too." He opened the door and pushed her through.

"Lock up if you need to," Shay said to him. "This is a tremendously rare opportunity."

"Hurry!"

Biting wind hit her in the face. Beneath the apron, she had on nothing warmer than the zip-up fitted sweatshirt she'd worn to work, but she couldn't think about a trifling thing like hypothermia at a time like this.

Misty River didn't have many claims to fame. The cinnamon rolls at Sugar Maple Kitchen. Fried chicken at The Junction. Polka Dot Apron Pies. And the Miracle Five.

Almost twenty years ago, five middle school kids from Misty River had been trapped underground by an earthquake while on a church mission trip to El Salvador. One of them, Luke Dempsey, had an early model cell phone with him. He called his parents and told them they were buried alive in the building's basement, but that his brother—who'd been right behind the others in the hallway when the earthquake struck—wasn't with them.

His parents had alerted news media and the story of the trapped kids had zoomed around the world—catching the hearts and concern of people in every country. Eight days later, a rescue team finally reached the kids and got them away safely because the wall protecting them did not fall. Later, engineers could not explain how that had occurred. By rights, the wall should have crashed, and they should have been crushed.

They'd been dubbed the Miracle Five.

Four of them—Natasha, Genevieve, Sebastian, and Ben—had toured for months afterward, telling their story to crowds of people. Books had been published about them. A hit movie had been released.

When Shay's mom had played that movie for her on their VCR, Shay had been mesmerized. Not only by the drama and inspiration of their story but by the astonishing fact that these world-famous kids were from Misty River. They were just a few years older than she was, in fact.

She'd been a fan ever since. Over the years, she'd spotted and even had the chance to talk with some of them. Natasha and Genevieve sometimes stopped by Papery as customers, which never failed to leave her starstruck.

The only one of them who'd immediately retreated from the spotlight was Luke. Understandably so. Luke's younger brother had not survived the tragedy and that loss had sent Luke on a path of destruction that had eventually landed him in jail for theft.

He'd been serving out his sentence for the past seven years. It had been big news in Misty River when he'd been released last month and returned to his hometown. Local gossip suggested that he was renovating his apartment on the upper floor of an industrial building a few blocks away. It was hard to know whether that was true because he was more reclusive than the Loch Ness Monster.

She'd *never* seen him this close. In fact, the last time she'd seen him had been when she was a kid and he'd crossed the street three cars in front of her mom's car. On that occasion, she'd suctioned herself to the front windshield like a gecko.

She trailed him as he turned off the square, walked half a block, and entered Rocky's Hardware Store. Feeling like detective Veronica Mars, she slowed, then slipped in after him. She glanced down each aisle the way she'd once done when searching for her mom in the grocery store.

There! She was pretty sure this was Luke. He appeared to be shopping for screws. She really wanted to meet his eyes, even for a split second. Doing so would allow her to confirm his identity and have a miniscule interaction with him.

She walked up the aisle adjacent to his. Gathering her nerve, she made her way around the endcap and down his aisle.

He gave no sign that he was aware of her presence. His head remained bent.

She pretended interest in the plungers, arrayed ten yards from him on the other side of the aisle. Covert side glance. He'd clothed his muscular body in jeans and a well-worn black leather jacket. He had dark brown hair, a profile of hard angles, scruff on his cheeks, and leave-me-alone body

66

language.

If he wanted to be left alone, how was she going to have a miniscule interaction with him? Inspiration struck and she knocked three of the plungers onto the floor.

At the clatter, he jerked. His head lifted.

"Sorry." She smiled at him.

Without smiling back, he returned his focus to the screws.

Shay set two of the plungers back in place and carried the third away, acting like a customer looking for additional items. Actually, she *was* a customer. Buying a plunger was the least she could do in the name of her cover story. One could never have too many plungers.

She texted Gabe as she walked. *It's absolutely Luke Dempsey. He entered Rocky's Hardware. Come IMMEDIATELY.* Gabe was as big a Miracle Five devotee as she was.

She took some deep breaths and shook out her legs. Luke's hazel eyes had been like the ice covering a lake. Cold and dangerous.

Gabe caught up to her, a little out of breath, in the hammer aisle.

She motioned for him to bend down so she could whisper in his ear. "He's super intimidating."

"Really?" Gabe appeared enthusiastic.

"Take a look at your own risk."

He ambled off and eventually met her at the cash register after she'd paid for her plunger. The door wheezed behind them as they exited. Together, they strode back toward Papery.

"That was so lucky," Shay said.

"I can't believe we just saw him in the flesh."

"It was a Christmas miracle."

"*Luke Dempsey.*" He shook his head. "Unbelievable."

"Did you find him intimidating?"

"Very."

"I think he might still be haunted by his brother's death."

"I wonder if he'll ever come inside the shop? That grief journal we carry has really helped some people."

"He didn't look to me like the stationery type, Gabe."

Two women stood outside Papery, sweetly waiting in response to the *Be back in five minutes!* message Gabe had taped to the locked door. It wasn't until after the women left—one with *Happy New Year!* cards because she'd given up on getting cards in the mail ahead of Christmas—that Gabe circled back to what they'd been discussing when she'd spotted Luke.

"You said earlier that I'd forgotten one hugely important obstacle between you and Connor," Gabe prompted.

"Connor asked me to be his dating consultant because he's interested in someone else. You warned me that some other woman was going to take him off the market if I didn't act. But the sad truth is, some other woman has already taken him off the market."

"Tell Connor how you're feeling. Maybe he'll rethink the other woman."

"Or maybe, if I tell him, that will only end up making him feel awkward around me." She continued into her office and lowered to her desk.

Who is Molly? Is she someone I know? And what had she done to inspire Connor to try so hard to please her?

Shay had had several boyfriends. Getting them had never been the issue. It was transitioning to love and lifelong commitment that had been the tough nut to crack. Pondering Connor's pursuit of Molly raised a depressing truth.

Connor was willing to spend the type of time and effort in pursuit of Molly that Shay's boy-friends had never been willing to spend in pursuit of her.

And now, in a display of terrible timing, she

was developing a crush on Connor right when he was about to confess his affection for someone else. Why hadn't she noticed his appeal sooner?

Regret heavy on her shoulders, she pulled out her phone and texted him. *I had a verified Luke Dempsey sighting just now.*

Seven minutes later, Connor replied. *Congratulations! Did you know that Ben Coleman is one of my teacher friends? I'd be happy to introduce you anytime.*

Ben was another member of the Miracle Five. Connor was willing to set up an introduction simply because he knew it would mean a lot to her.

See? Connor was good.

"Wouldn't it be nice to date someone who's just good, without fine print?" Gabe had asked. It would be nice. At what point was she going to grow up and start choosing men who were great for her?

Not at this point, apparently, since Connor was off-limits.

I'd be delighted to meet Ben, thank you. She followed that with another text a few seconds later. *Do you remember the dating strategies you and I discussed yesterday?*

We discussed that, if I listen to Molly, I'll get a grasp on what types of activities she enjoys. In Molly's case, she enjoys ice skating at Christmastime. So, I can simply

ask, "Would you like to go out with me sometime?"
Then suggest that we go ice skating.

Precisely! Ice skating is a good choice because there
can be a lot of pressure associated with spending a
first date sitting across a table from someone. This
way, you'll have an activity to think and talk about. If
the ice skating goes well, you could see if she wants to
grab a coffee from the stand beside the rink. But only
if it's going well. If it's not, go your separate ways and
reassess.

Got it. Can you and I practice the ice-skating date
soon?

Tomorrow after work? I can meet you at the high
school.

If so, I'll introduce you to Ben.

It's a (pretend) date! See you then.

Chapter Five

At the appointed time, Shay turned in to the parking lot of Misty River High School. The lot had cleared out significantly, but not totally, at this hour on a Friday.

She enjoyed staying at least slightly connected with her alma mater. In the spring, she always set up a Papery booth at the high school's fundraising farmers market. In the fall, she made it a point to attend a handful of the home football games.

Whenever she returned to campus, a landslide of memories greeted her. Her brother, peeling onto the main road on those rare and precious occasions when he'd taken her, Ash, and Danielle off campus for lunch. How she'd felt, waiting on the starting line of a cross country meet, her anticipation and adrenaline buzzing. The beloved red dress she'd worn to the Midwinter Dance her senior year, and how she and Nicolas had slow danced to "Just the Way You Are" by Bruno Mars.

She parked and observed a trio of girls talking and laughing as they crossed in front of her. They were so young! They were experiencing what Shay had once experienced on this campus. She felt linked to them and, at the same time, separate from them. They were going to the school she'd attended, but the campus and the staff and the world had changed since then.

She walked in the direction of the beige brick administrative building, where Connor had suggested they meet.

Today, gauzy clouds hunkered low against hills arching into cold, pale blue sky. These Blue Ridge mountains were more than her literal home. They were the home of her heart. Though her family situation had long been hard, the place in which she'd been raised had always been right.

She spotted Connor before he saw her. He wore some of his new clothing. The beige twill shirt open over a black T-shirt. Jeans. His gray jacket.

Her heart tugged toward him even as her rational self tugged it back. She could not jump from a romance with Nate the Disappointment straight into a doomed infatuation with Connor. *No thank you, self-destruction.*

She recognized the man chatting with Connor

as Ben Coleman of the Miracle Five. Ben had closely cropped black hair and a warm brown skin tone. He'd been a stand-out baseball player in high school and college. Nowadays, he taught eleventh grade science, yet he still carried himself like an athlete. His family was one of the most well-known in town. Large and loving and boisterous—the type of family she'd always wished she had.

Connor raised a hand to her in greeting and smiled with what looked like genuine pleasure.

She'd told him when they started this process that she was simply shining the diamond. The minor exterior changes she'd made so far had already shined the diamond to brilliance. She'd continue to help him to the best of her ability, even though doing so would lift him out of her league. By the time this was all said and done, she'd be the one asking him if he could be her consultant because she was going to be the one sitting at home on Friday and Saturday nights, and he was going to be the one using a cattle prod to keep women away.

"Shay," Connor said when she reached them, "this is Ben Coleman. Ben, Shay Seaver."

"It's so nice to meet you," Shay said to Ben just as a blond woman joined their group.

Ben's posture tightened subtly.

"And this is Leah Montgomery," Connor said, nodding to the blonde. "She teaches the school's most advanced math students. Trust me when I say she's very impressive. A genius."

"If only my students found me impressive," Leah said wryly to Shay.

Was this Molly? If Connor had fallen for someone at work, that would make sense. He spent a lot more time here than he did out in social situations. And Leah was lovely . . . very much so. Intelligent blue-gray eyes were the highlight of her delicate face. Side-parted hair fell in loose waves to her jaw line.

"It's a pleasure to meet you," Leah said to Shay. "Connor has told us so much about you."

"He has?" Shay asked with surprise.

"He has," Ben answered. "Any friend of Connor's is a friend of ours."

"Very true," Leah said.

"As long as I've known Shay," Connor said, "and that's a long time because we met in middle school, she's been a fan of the Miracle Five."

"I've read the books," Shay said to Ben, "and countless articles. I've seen the movie a dozen times. Your story inspires me. It reminds me that miracles still happen, and that God is still as active as He ever was."

"Amen." Lines of kindness lightly marked the skin beside his eyes. "We spend too much of our time trying to control things that aren't ours to control. The rescue taught me that God can be trusted. You'd think, seeing as how I lived through it, that I wouldn't have to remind myself of that lesson so often." He shrugged. "But I still do."

Several teen girls passed, shooting Connor and Ben dazzled looks.

Shay asked Ben a few questions about his work and his family.

Ben was known as the optimistic one of the five and she saw evidence of that in spades.

The only off-key note? A faintly stilted vibe between Ben and Leah, despite their friendliness. Connor had told Shay that he'd worked with Ben and Leah for the past few years. They all knew each other well and liked each other a lot. So, why the undercurrent of stiffness?

When she and Connor parted from Leah and Ben, two young female teachers immediately waylaid Connor. The women made googly eyes at him and agreed with everything he said.

Just as she'd expected, Connor had a large fan club here. She couldn't decide whether to feel smug or sad.

When the women moved off, they began walking toward their cars. "Is Leah Molly?" she asked outright.

His gait stuttered. "No."

"Would you tell me if she was?"

"Yes. Leah loves Sebastian Grant."

"*What?*" Sebastian was another of the Miracle Five.

"Yeah, Leah and Sebastian. They're a couple."

Leah wasn't Molly, Lord be praised. "I could be wrong, but I noticed something strange between Leah and Ben just now. An underlying . . . hesitation."

"Ben fell for Leah as soon as she came to work here. He and Leah are close, but her feelings for him have always been platonic. Then she met Sebastian and her feelings for him weren't platonic." He shot her a look, one eyebrow raised. "It got complicated."

"Oh no." It was widely known that Ben and Sebastian were best friends. "So Sebastian started dating Leah even though Ben found her first?"

"Only after Ben gave him full permission to do so. By that point, Ben knew that it wasn't going to happen for him and Leah."

"Has Ben and Sebastian's relationship fractured? If so, I'm not going to be okay."

"Their relationship's intact. They all behaved

honorably. They all care about each other. It's just that this only went down less than two months ago so it's still a little sensitive."

"Has it been strange for you, to be in a friend group with Leah and Ben? Since they're in a weird place?"

"At times, yes. I'll be glad when Ben finds someone. He's great."

"Connor!" Yet another female teacher around their age flagged him down.

Shay hid a groan. It seemed Connor was already out of her league. Men did not stop her every thirty feet when she tried to walk from her job to her car.

Had Connor ever been in her league? He lived in Misty River because he was helping his mom through ALS. She was a skilled stationery designer, but he was a phenomenal painter. He was kind, a good listener, a man who worked with teens, a man who was seeking the advice of a dating consultant in order to win Molly's heart.

● ● ●

Misty River's temporary ice rink operated from the weekend before Thanksgiving to the weekend after New Year's thanks to technology that kept it mechanically frozen even on warmer days. The rink's short timeframe had never been a problem for Connor because he'd only skated twice before in his life. Both times had been a disaster. He hadn't been tempted to skate since.

He'd hoped to make progress with Shay by spending time with her and by making adjustments according to her taste. She loved to ice skate and she'd advised him to invite Molly out on an activity Molly loved for their first date. So here he was.

Any chance, though, that he was gutting potential progress with Shay by trying on stretchy pants in front of her and showing her how bad he was at ice skating?

They carried their rented skates to one of the benches facing the rink and bent to lace them. The town of Misty River had installed the rink on a small parking lot, bordered on three sides by a park. On the parking lot side, they'd added a booth for tickets and skate rental, seating, area heaters, and a coffee truck.

"It's fortunate for me that Molly loves to ice skate," Shay said, "because as it happens, I also love to ice skate."

"Oh?" he said neutrally.

"Yep. I love skating! My grandma used to bring us a few times every winter."

He frowned at the rink. The ice looked deceptively pretty and the people skating smoothly around the oval made it look deceptively easy. There was a reason he hadn't become a hockey player. In fact, there was a reason why he'd poured all his time and skill into art instead of sports in general.

He worked out five days a week on the rowing machine in the basement. A few times a year he went on an adventure race with his uncle and cousins—where they'd spend days in the wilderness using navigation, hiking, and paddling to make their way through a course.

Rowing machines and adventure races—the most coordinated things he could manage.

Shay, on the other hand, was a born athlete. It was one of the things he'd always admired about her. She was tough enough to push through the pain of running. Disciplined enough to train.

He wasn't surprised when she sailed several feet onto the ice. She'd dressed in waterproof pants and a sporty white jacket. Her striped pastel scarf, hat, and mittens all matched. Her hair peeked out symmetrically from the bottom of the cap.

He eased onto the ice, arms outstretched, ankles straight. He slid about ten inches.

She waited, but he didn't make a move.

"Is that a skating posture I'm unaware of?" she asked kindly. "The scarecrow, perhaps?"

"I probably should have mentioned at the beginning that I'm not good at this. I can stand here but I've never been able to figure out how to make myself move forward without falling."

"Understandable. But this pretend date is not going to be very enjoyable for you if you remain in that position the entire time." She smiled.

"It strikes me that maybe I should take . . . Molly out to do things that she enjoys *and* that I'm good at." Kids jostled past him to exit the ice.

"Not necessarily. If Molly's worth her salt, she's going to be willing to try things that you enjoy but she's not good at. So you should be willing to do the same for her. We'll make our lives small if we never attempt anything in support of the people we care about."

"I agree in theory." *Crap, this ice is so slippery.*

"How about you keep one hand on the handrail? That's what I did when I was starting out."

He edged to the side, took hold of the handrail, and moved his feet like he was walking. No gliding here. Just walking on ice wearing skates.

She skated beside him at his snail's pace. "Try pushing one skate to the side and skimming forward on the other."

To please her, he tried, lost his footing, and yanked on the arm gripping the rail. A few more minutes dragged past. He didn't like to call attention to himself, but his bad skating was doing just that. "This can't be fun for you," he said. Thank God she hadn't spent her money on this outing. He'd convinced her that he would pay— seeing as how she was here as his consultant. "Don't let me hold you back. Please skate around as fast as you want."

She seemed to understand. "'Kay. I'll skate for fifteen minutes or so and then check back to see if you want to try it with me."

"Thanks."

She soared off, lapping him again and again. His feet kept shooting out from under him, yanking his arm. The handrail was the only thing saving him from a butt fracture. *Yank*. Nonetheless, he kept trying—*yank*—because he'd agreed with what she'd said. His life would become small if he never attempted anything in support of the people he cared about.

He cared about her. Also, skating did come with one perk. Watching Shay.

She radiated happiness. Her body was lithe and strong. The wind whipped through the tips of her hair. At one point, he spotted her turning circles in the middle of the rink, arms outstretched.

He stopped, spellbound.

As always, she was doing her thing, unconcerned with what others thought.

She was beautiful to him. She, who was so many of the things he wasn't, had always been beautiful to him. *And I'd do anything—even this— to spend time with her.*

Sunset was arriving and the string lights mounted overhead blinked to life. He could see why so many Christmas movies included ice-skating scenes. The setting was the type of thing women liked. Sadly for him, he could also see why those movies didn't show the hero strangling the handrail or venturing out onto the ice and toppling over like a baby giraffe. Not the type of thing women liked.

True to her word, Shay swirled to a stop in front of him after fifteen minutes. "How are you doing, Brian Boitano?"

He laughed.

She grinned, her brown eyes bright.

"I'm almost ready for the Olympic trials," he said.

"How about I try to pull you forward, very slowly and carefully?"

"That's a generous offer, but I'm worried that

if I leave the handrail, I'll fall and pull you down with me."

"I'm willing to take that risk." She extended her mittens to him.

He let go of the handrail and linked his hands with hers. Heat spread from the contact. This was the first time they'd held hands.

She started weaving her skates in an hourglass type of motion. She faced backward, he faced forward. She was going ninety percent slower than she'd been going, but he was now going fifty percent faster than he'd been going.

Don't fall. Don't fall. He set his jaw in concentration.

He fell.

As predicted, he took her down with him. The force of the impact on the hard ice jarred through him. She landed facing him, looking startled by the crash.

The only thing that could make this date worse? If one of them was obligated to take the other to the emergency room.

"I'm so sorry," he said. "Are you okay?"

Her whole face scrunched and then she was belly laughing.

The sound was contagious. The two of them sat on the ice, skaters flowing around them, laughing until Shay's eyes grew wet with amusement.

She was fine. And for the next few seconds he could take a break from trying not to fall.

"You warned me that might happen," she eventually said, making no attempt to rise. "And I accepted the risk, so I bear responsibility. I am very glad that we went on this test date."

"Me too."

"We've learned that while it certainly is important to try things in support of the people you care about, ice skating may not be the best bet for your first date with Molly, after all. You seem to be having to grit your teeth to get through this."

"By the time this is over I won't have any teeth left."

She gave another peal of laughter. "I will tell you, though, that it can be very attractive, from a woman's perspective, to see a man persevering at something he's not naturally skilled at. You've done this with such a good attitude and a sense of humor. That will go far with Molly."

"Do you think she'll still like me if I only have a mouth full of empty gums?"

She hadn't stopped smiling.

He was almost certainly over-reaching with Shay. It wasn't that he'd ever felt he deserved her.

It's just that he'd wanted her so much for so long that he'd been compelled to act.

He still believed in the overall merit of this dating-consultant ploy. The night of the Christmas tree lighting, he'd told her there was a woman he really liked (true) and that he wanted to keep the woman's identity a secret (temporarily true). Shay was the one who'd given Molly a name. Shay had logically determined Shay wasn't her. But perpetuating that untruth was making him more and more uncomfortable. He'd started this for the greater good. However, deception wasn't in his nature, and he was starting to have doubts.

How much longer should he let this go on? Christmas was two weeks away. He'd definitely end it before then, as planned.

"When you're on your date with Molly," she said, "I want you two to do something that enables you to have fun, too."

"This is not that."

"Agreed."

"I'm going to crawl over to the exit of the rink now—"

Another snort of laughter from her.

"—but I'd like you to skate as long as you want. That would make me feel better about dragging you all the way out here."

"I've never been one to skate for hours. I'll go for a little bit longer, and that'll be enough."

"I'll wait for you, but no hurry. I have some things I need to check on my phone."

"I'm guessing checking things on your phone is preferable to this?"

"Anything on dry land, including having surgery, would be preferable to this."

"If you attempt any more skating, surgery might become a possibility for you." A dimple dug into her cheek as she adjusted her scarf.

"Can I buy you coffee when you're done, to pay you back for this debacle?"

"Certainly. I take payment for my consultation services in the form of rented ice skates and gingerbread lattes."

• • •

An hour later, Shay let herself into her matchbox apartment and set about unwrapping her winter layers and getting dinner going. Frozen enchiladas—dinner of champions.

Connor Bryant was the worst ice skater she'd ever seen in her life. Comically bad. However, she hadn't been lying when she'd told him that his good attitude on the ice could appeal to Molly. She knew for a fact it could, because that's the effect it'd had on her.

He hadn't lost his temper or his cool. He'd been able to laugh at himself and remained genuinely good-natured the whole time. With his auburn coloring, the cold had brought out red patches near his cheekbones, which had made him look extremely hot in a British rugby player kind of way.

But the most slaying thing about their date— *pretend* date—was that he'd been willing to subject himself to ice skating for Molly.

Dang it!

Once again, he'd proven he'd go the extra mile.

Numerous times tonight, she'd wondered if Connor was picking up on the very tangible chemistry between her and him. Each time, she'd decided that no, he wasn't. She'd observed him interacting with the women at his school, and he'd appeared oblivious to their interest. No doubt he was equally oblivious to the electricity she was feeling.

After all, they'd known each other a long time. Nothing had changed between herself and Connor except one thing—her emotions toward him. "'Can you feel the love tonight?'" She sang the *Lion King* lyric under her breath.

She'd signed up for this project so blithely. In

88

doing so, she'd gotten herself into a predicament. She was beginning to harbor legit jealousy toward Molly, a woman whose identity she didn't even know.

Merry Christmas to you, Shay. Merry Christmas to you.

Chapter Six

Only a day had passed since they'd gone ice skating. To Shay, it felt like a week.

She sat cross-legged on her sofa Saturday evening after returning home from a holiday dinner out with friends. Steadily, she chewed kernels of the peppermint and white chocolate popcorn a customer had given her while she watched a televised stage production of *White Christmas*.

It really did feel like a week since she'd seen Connor. Fine! She'd text him.

Brushing off her hands, she selected her words the way a stationery lover selects greeting cards.

Here's another low-pressure first date idea... You could invite Molly to go to a party or gathering at which both of you will know people. She sent the text, then tapped her phone against her chin.

Could Molly be Bridget, who worked at the art gallery? Shay and Connor had chatted with her when they'd stopped by the other day. Shay had detected some shy interest on Bridget's part but hadn't detected anything unusual in Connor's behavior. That didn't mean Bridget wasn't Molly. Bridget was darling in an "I'm an elf from *Lord of the Rings*" way. Connor and Bridget shared an appreciation of art. No doubt, Bridget would think Connor was a prodigy and Connor would be grateful to date someone who thought he was a prodigy.

She, Shay, thought he was a prodigy!

Her phone pinged with his answering text. *After our ice-skating fiasco, I hope you can agree that I'm going to need more practice at selecting and executing good dates. My friend Andrew invited me to an ugly Christmas sweater party at his house tomorrow night. Is that the kind of thing you think Molly would enjoy?*

> *I can't speak to Molly's tastes. But I can tell you that I think parties are a good bet, so long as she's familiar with some of the people who are going. Is it Andrew Covington who's hosting?*
>
> *Yep.*

Like her, Connor had gone through middle school and high school with just a couple of very close friends. Like her, it appeared he'd retained them to this day. Andrew had been their gangly salutatorian and now had his own small IT business. He was the one she'd hired for all Papery's tech needs.

I don't want to impose on your time, Connor wrote, *but would you be willing to go to Andrew's party with me for an hour or two? I'd like a chance to prove to you and myself that I really am ready for this.*

She smiled, warmth circling like glitter in her chest. She had an event at church on her calendar, but she could easily miss that. *Do you have to grit your teeth in order to survive ugly Christmas sweater parties?*

As a rule, I don't enjoy dressing in embarrassing clothing, as you may have noticed the day of the stretchy pants. But Andrew's promised that there won't be embarrassing games or forced caroling. It'll be low-key. Just food and talking to people. So I don't think I'll have to grit my teeth to survive.

In that case, my answer is yes.

●　　●　　●

Once again, Shay was seeing him at less than his sexiest. His sweater read *Dachshund through the snow* and had a picture of a dachshund wearing a Santa hat on the front. It was the least hideous one he'd been able to find. But it wasn't great. How were you supposed to bring your A game with a woman when wearing a *Dachshund through the snow* sweater?

Her sweater was much louder than his. Made to look like a Christmas tree, its bright green fabric had actual tinsel and ornaments hanging off of it. She wore matching Christmas ornaments as earrings. But, of course, the laws of the universe dictated that she'd look adorable and confident in her sweater. Which she did.

Christmas music, bursts of laughter, and the conversation of the guests ebbed and flowed around them like the tide.

"There's an art to attending a party with a date," she was saying to him.

"I'm all ears."

"If it seems that Molly isn't comfortable with you leaving her side, then by all means, stay next to her as you mingle. But if she becomes engrossed, for example, in a conversation with one of her friends, it's perfectly cool to give her space. There's sizzle in meeting the eyes of someone you're attracted to from across the room." She pointed to the food and drinks. "Say you go get a holiday drink. While you're there, you could lift a cup and ask her wordlessly if she wants one. Or you could be talking to guys fifteen feet away and give her a secret smile."

"To be honest, I don't know what a secret

smile is."

"It's the kind of smile you give someone when you share a secret. In this case, the secret you share is that you like one another and that the night holds fabulous potential."

"Not sure I can convey all that with a smile."

"Like so." She glanced up at him out of the corners of her eyes, lips tilting. Their gazes locked for only a split second before she looked away, but the contact packed power.

Need stole his breath.

"I know several people here," she continued, "so how about you go hang out with your friends and we'll practice? If at any moment Molly—in this case me—looks like she's been stranded, excuse yourself and return to her. But if it looks like she's having a fabulous time, then don't feel obligated to do so. On the other hand, don't stay away from her *so* long that she thinks, *Why did he invite me here? He's not spending any time with me.*"

His head spun. "I see what you mean about this being an art form. Just . . . not the form of art I've mastered."

"Which is why we're taking this on a test run." She moved off, easily finding people to chat with. Around town, she was well-known and well-liked.

Much more so than he was.

Connor crossed to Andrew. At first it felt awkward, trying to do all the things she'd mentioned. But he soon realized it wasn't hard at all. He was crazy about Shay. Whenever he'd been in a room with her for the past sixteen years, his attention had strayed to her. So he'd just let it do what it wanted to do.

Sometimes when he looked her way, she didn't meet his eyes. Which was fine because at all times he could tell she was doing great. She wasn't stranded. When their gazes did intersect, he felt the warm jolt of it like a physical touch.

In time, he returned to her, and she excused herself from her conversation to pull him to the side of the room.

"How did I do?" he asked.

"Connor, you did so, *so* well. Really! *A*+! Was that less painful than ice skating?"

"Infinitely so."

• • •

The following day at work, Shay caught herself staring into space, reliving the ugly sweater party.

Shay. You're supposed to be fulfilling website orders. Adroitly, she taped closed a padded envelope, flipped it over, and then . . . went still as her thoughts tugged her back to the party.

It had been a revelation! Restrained Connor had been a master of across-the-room attraction. Shared glances. Shared smiles. His focus returning to her again and again. Who'd have guessed?

Quiet intensity lived in him. It was easy to miss, at first. But once you saw it, it was impossible to ignore. He was a composed man and his composure called to her. But beneath that composure lay passion and deep emotion. She was sure of it. And that called to her even more loudly.

She'd felt a delicious crackle when he'd looked at her from across Andrew's living room.

Her phone dinged, interrupting her reverie.

I've completed another painting, Connor texted. *I'd love for you to come over and name it when you have time.*

Her fingers flew as she typed her reply. *I respond to artwork naming needs almost as quickly as Batman responds to the bat signal. I'll swing by tomorrow after work.*

• • •

"Shay!" Penny Bryant said as she swung open the door to their bungalow. "Will you look at that snow!"

"I know." Snowflakes drifted soundlessly toward the thin blanket of snow accumulating on the ground. "It's gorgeous."

"Come in. I sent Connor to the grocery store for more sugar, but he'll be back any minute."

Warmth and the scent of chocolate surrounded her as she stepped inside.

"How is my nativity angel doing?" Penny asked.

"Cherubic? Serene?"

"Excellent, excellent." Penny waved for Shay to follow her toward the kitchen.

Over the past week, Shay had been added to an email loop concerning the nativity and had completed a fitting with the costume mistress. Apparently, that was all the preparation needed because she only had to show up at the right place and time, then stand there, looking angelic.

The Vine Church choir had sung at the Christmas tree lighting, so, in order to prevent a turf war, the Baptists would sing Christmas hymns at the nativity. Volunteers would handle the animals, the set, the lighting, the printing of the pamphlets about the Christmas story, and the table serving free cider and cookies.

"I'm making homemade hot chocolate," Penny announced, taking up a position in front of the stove and stirring the contents of a saucepan with a wooden spoon. "I was thrilled when I heard that you were going to stop by because I only allow myself to make this on the days in December when people stop by. Will you drink some?"

"Absolutely."

"I'm so pleased that you and Connor have been spending time together lately."

"Me too."

"He's lonely."

Shay's stomach dropped. "Oh?"

"He's not a complainer and he hides it well. But yes. I worry that he's lonely." She added ingredients and continued to stir. "This is my mother's recipe. It calls for milk, cocoa, sugar, chocolate chips, and vanilla. There's no substitute for homemade."

"I can't think of a time when I've had home-made hot chocolate."

"Then you're in for a treat." She winked, sampled the drink with a spoon, and placed the spoon in the sink.

"Can you . . . elaborate a little more on what's going on with Connor?" Shay asked.

"He has a full life. His job, his family, his friends. But it's a unique road he's traveling, as my caregiver. I don't know a single person in his circle who's in the same boat as he is. He's in his boat alone."

"I understand."

"He loves art. But he spends every spare minute in that studio. I don't believe that's purely because he loves it. I think he's trying to fill the hours. And maybe process his emotions? His sorrow over my health. His heartbreak."

"Heartbreak?"

"He reminds me sometimes of a person who's given their heart away and now their heart's living outside their body." Penny poured hot chocolate into two matching Christmas mugs. "Here you are."

Shay accepted her mug and they sat opposite one another at the kitchen table.

"It's not as sweet as it should be because I didn't have quite enough sugar," Penny said. "Which is why I sent Connor on an emergency grocery store run."

Shay took a sip. It was like drinking a chocolate bar. "It's perfect." *If it were any sweeter it would be syrup.* "I do agree that Connor has given his heart away."

Penny set down her mug. "Yes. To you?"

The question took Shay aback. Her perceptions shifted slightly on their axis. His mom thought Connor had given his heart to *her*? "No. To someone else." Wait. Was she Molly?

No. That was wishful thinking. If she was Molly, Connor would simply have asked her out. He wouldn't have gone to the trouble of a ruse like this.

Penny looked perplexed. "He gave his heart to someone else? Who?"

"He hasn't told me. I'm helping him prepare, though, to ask her out."

"Mm," Penny murmured in an unconvinced tone.

Had there been a time in the past when Connor liked her? She wished she'd noticed! And yet . . . She had to cut herself some slack. She'd been a kid. Her taste in boys had been haywire. "Why did you think it was me who he'd given his heart to?"

"He was enamored with you when you were younger."

"He was? He told you that?"

"He's never been the type to confide in me about romance. But I could tell he adored you. It was all over his face. More than once, I drove him to cross country meets when you were running. That was back in the day before he had his own license."

"Really? I had no idea."

Just then, she heard the front door open and close.

Connor entered the kitchen from the hallway.

He was dressed more casually than usual, in track pants and a long-sleeved athletic tee. A slow, tender smile moved across his mouth as he took her in. "Hey."

In response, desire curled through Shay like a satin ribbon. "Hi."

"More sugar," Connor said to his mom, setting a grocery bag on the counter.

"Thank you, darling. Hot chocolate?"

"I'll have some later."

"Were your ears burning?" Penny asked him. "My nativity angel and I were just talking about you."

His brows immediately lowered with concern.

"It was all good," Shay hurried to say.

"Your nativity angel is actually here to christen my new painting," Connor said to his mom.

"Yes," Penny answered, "but nativity angels always have time to chat with their doting librarians in the world."

"And they never say no to chocolate," Shay added. "What's your role in the nativity?" Shay asked Connor.

"This year I'm one of the people who passes out food."

"What?" she squawked. "How come you're not a shepherd or Joseph?"

"Because only my mom's naive new recruits agree to be character actors."

"Connor!" Penny chastised with fake outrage.

"It's true," he said to Shay.

Apparently, she was a pawn in Penny's master nativity plan.

"Shay," Penny said, "while you finish your hot chocolate, I'd like to hear all about your stationery shop."

Shay explained that Christmas fever had reached dizzying heights in Misty River and that she and Gabe were doing their best to radiate holiday cheer while working overtime.

She didn't tell them that, in her heart of hearts, a discordant note kept ringing. She looked forward to spending time with her brother and sister-in-law on Christmas Eve, but Christmas Day would be fraught with tension thanks to her parents. Nate the Disappointment was gone. Her feelings toward Connor were fruitless. So this particular Christmas was shaping up to be sadder than most.

Shay! Look at Penny and Connor! A grave diagnosis hung over them and they weren't griping. She had a lot to be thankful for. Wonderful friends. Her business. That was enough for any person.

During recent talks with Connor, she'd learned

that though his sisters could be loud and challenging, they were also as good-hearted as Connor and his mom. These two could expect a warm, rowdy, loving Christmas. Which was no less than they deserved.

The discordant note rang again, stubborn. However, it was scientifically impossible for a person to give in to depression when drinking a chocolate bar.

She arrived at Connor's studio, once again, with the taste of chocolate in her mouth. Reverently, she approached the newly finished piece while snow floated down as perfectly as if it had been manufactured for the Broadway production of *Frozen*.

He'd chosen colors similar to those of the last piece, except that he'd added one new shade—somewhere between peach and dusky pink. The work communicated emotion to her. Longing.

She spent time composing possible titles in her head. "To me, this one is like looking at love's garden through a frosted window."

Several seconds of quiet followed. She turned her chin to him and found that his attention was on her.

"Love's Garden Through a Frosted Window is the perfect title," he said.

"Were you channeling love with this one?"

He shifted from one foot to the other. "I was. Thank you for the title."

"We angels aim to please." She neared the shelves, idly running a fingertip down his various tools, visualizing them in his calm, capable hands as he worked.

She earnestly wished she could stay, but checking her watch, she saw she'd need to leave in a few minutes. She loved this studio, this house, time spent with him. In Connor's presence, she felt two things that she typically didn't feel simultaneously with guys. She felt valued. And she felt physical magnetism.

Back when her parents' marriage tanked, she'd realized that pleasing them had become impossible. She'd forsaken that goal and instead decided to claim her individuality, to please herself. Sometimes, she rubbed people the wrong way. They viewed her as too independent, too outspoken, too individual, too quick to stick up for herself or her business.

With Connor, it was like a vacation because she didn't have to worry about that. He accepted her. More than that, he seemed to appreciate her.

He was starting to feel like home to her . . . yet she couldn't let that sensation take root. He wasn't. Her boyfriend. Or her home. "What attracted you to Molly?" she asked.

"Her confidence. She knew her own mind."

"How long have you liked her?"

"Quite a while."

"What's stopped you from asking her out before now?"

"At first, I was too shy to do it. Lately, circumstances."

"How much do you like her?"

"This much." He indicated the painting. He'd said he'd been channeling love while working on it.

He loved Molly. The admission pierced her with the chill of a metal stake. "Your mom told me that she drove you to some of my cross country meets before you were old enough to drive. Did you go to the meets . . . for me?"

He hesitated. "Yeah."

"You never mentioned you were there."

"We were friends and I liked to cheer for my friends. But I never liked to"—he shrugged—"publicize it."

She wanted to throw herself into his arms and kiss him. He was irresistible. And she felt such a powerful pang of remorse that she hadn't given him the time of day back when he'd liked her, that she needed to go. "I have to run. I'm on my way to a Christmas cookie exchange."

"Sure. Thanks again."

Leave, Shay! She walked to the door, stopping before the threshold even though she hadn't intended to do so. She glanced back. "If things are going well between you and Molly after date one and date two, it's likely that she might invite you over to her place."

"You think?"

"I really do. So, I'm standing in for Molly and inviting you over to . . . eat pizza and watch a Christmas movie. That way, you'll be able to do a dry run. And up your game when you go to Molly's." What was she doing? Was she embracing self-destruction with both arms? Yes. Yes, she was. "When are you available between now and the live nativity?"

"Sunday night."

"That night's good for me. I'll text my address."

"Shay."

She waited.

He slid his hands in his pockets as was his habit. An artist, in his gorgeous studio, surrounded by his paintings. "Any advice for me? About what to do when and if Molly invites me to her apartment?"

"Act pleased but not too pleased."

"Clear as mud."

She chuckled. "It's never a bad idea to bring a hostess gift. I'm more of a plant person, but most women would be delighted with flowers. If she's making dinner, you could bring dessert. If she's making dessert, you could offer to bring dinner. And, of course, any woman always appreciates the gift of stationery."

"So . . . when I come over to your place on Sunday, I'll bring dessert."

"When you come over to my place, we'll just be practicing, so you don't need to bring anything. I have more peppermint popcorn than we can eat. I'm ordering pizza. And I already own a whole shop full of stationery."

• • •

Two days later, Gabe pulled free the "18" drawer on their house-shaped advent calendar. His eyes rounded when he saw four pieces of Hubba Bubba gum inside. "*Yes!* My favorite."

"For you to enjoy during your after-work hours." She'd outlawed Hubba Bubba during work because he was such an obnoxious smacker.

He thanked her and held the gum up to his nose, smiling as he inhaled the scent of pink

107

sweetness.

"You're a very strange person. At times, I wonder what I was thinking when I hired you."

"Liar. You've never wondered what you were thinking when you hired me. I'm the best thing to happen to Papery since . . . you."

She tidied a display of Christmas cocktail napkins.

"Have you told Connor how you feel about him yet?" Gabe asked, keeping the gum near his nose for a few more whiffs.

"Nope. Day before yesterday he indicated that he loves Molly."

"No!"

"Yes. At the moment, my best plan is to bide my time and see what happens between the two of them."

"And if things go badly, you'll swoop in and take advantage of his heartbreak?"

"Well, yes. Just not in such crass terms."

He tucked the gum into his apron pocket. "Your plan stinks."

"This whole situation stinks! I've spent most of December helping the man I like win the heart of a woman he likes. I really wish I would've woken up to his appeal sooner, back when he was available."

"The heart's timetable is a mystery," he said

philosophically. "You're late to the party but I still think you should go ahead and tell Connor now."

"I can't!"

"You can. Now is the most natural time, because you've been spending a lot of time with him, having a lot of conversations."

"Not *that* conversation. All our efforts have been focused on giving him the best chance at a happy relationship with Molly. I'm not going to destroy those efforts by coming in between them now."

One of their most challenging customers, Mrs. Grippo, shuffled into the store. She stopped by often, mostly to complain about how expensive their products were before leaving disgruntled.

Shay snuck toward her office. "Time for me to return to work on the new line of notepads," she whispered.

"Don't you dare," he murmured.

"Oh, I do dare. You might be a foot and a half taller than me, but you're all bark and no bite."

Chapter Seven

Connor spent way too long getting ready for dinner at Shay's apartment. He wasn't planning to tell her that she was Molly tonight and yet it had still taken him ages to shower, shave, and second-guess which clothes to wear before settling on his rust-colored sweater, jeans, and chukka boots. He'd tried to do something with his hair before remembering Shay mentioning at some point that she liked it "casual." Gratefully, he'd left it alone and gone to the nursery. But then more doubt had met him. What kind of plant to buy? What kind of planter?

Suddenly, simple decisions weren't so simple. Tonight meant a lot to him. He didn't want to mess it up.

He ended up having to speed from the nursery to her apartment in order to arrive on time. He caught a string of green lights and knocked on her door slightly out of breath.

The door swung back. "Hi," she said.

Like always, it took him a moment to adjust to the dazzling sight of her. She wasn't wearing athletic clothing today. Instead, she'd chosen a pale pink fuzzy sweater and a pair of jeans that hugged the shape of her hips and legs. "Hi."

Her vision flitted to his gift, then back to his face. "What's this?" she asked with pleased surprise.

"A white African violet. For you."

She accepted the medium-sized stone pot. "Thank you. You really didn't have to bring anything."

Except, I did. You suggested I bring Molly a gift and you're Molly. "I know." He followed her into an apartment that smelled like pine, due to the real Christmas tree in the corner.

An invitation to her place was worth more to him than an invitation to the treasure cave in *Aladdin*. He entered, filled with curiosity.

Her apartment was sophisticated, furnished in the same bright pastels and creamy whites of her shop. Organized. Modern. Tasteful. If he'd been shown a photo of this apartment in a lineup, he'd have known it was hers. It suited her perfectly, which meant he liked it instantly.

"How did I do with the plant?" he asked. "Did

I go too small? Too big? Choose the wrong kind of flowers?"

"Back at the ugly Christmas sweater party, your instincts were right on the money. Once again, they're right on the money. Not only did you hear me when I said I'm more of a plant person, but you chose a planter that jives with my style." She set the pot on the center of her table. "It's perfect."

She took his coat, asked if he wanted something to drink, then showed him around. Shay made just about everything she did look easy, and hosting him in her home was no different. She was comfortable in herself, and her relaxed demeanor loosened the tension that had knotted his neck muscles on the drive over.

She pulled a pizza box out of the oven where she'd been keeping it warm, and they sat in front of the two fancy place settings she'd arranged. He ate pepperoni, bell pepper, mushroom, and olive pizza off a china plate. He used a fabric napkin and drank water out of something that looked like a martini glass.

Her hair slipped over the shoulders of her sweater. The sound of her laughter resonated deep inside him. A tiny heart-shaped charm on a necklace rested between her collarbones against flawless skin.

Connor's gaze kept returning to that charm and he had to remind himself not to stare. Not at the charm. Or her lips, or too deeply into her eyes.

Shay was brave, uninhibited, determined. Many times a day, he remembered her at the ice rink, arms outstretched as she'd spun.

They'd been together a lot this month. After this, if she didn't want him, he couldn't tell himself it was because he hadn't had enough time with her. Objectively, he'd had enough time with her. If he couldn't convince her to give him a chance after he'd hung out with her all month, following her advice, cutting his hair, and buying new clothes, then he wasn't going to be able to convince her.

So why did it feel like it hadn't been enough? Like he hadn't done enough?

All he knew for sure was that he couldn't let those concerns stop him. He needed to reveal his hand to Shay. Soon. He'd never been so aware of the clock, ticking off time. He'd taken this story about Molly as far as he could. It had expired.

If Shay turned him down, he'd find a way to let go of the dream of her that had been part of the fabric of him for the majority of his life. The thought rang hollow in his chest.

After dinner, they moved to the sofa. Her tree

113

glittered, its silhouette reflected in the windows that framed a peaceful nighttime view of their town.

"We're the same age." She set a circular metal tub of popcorn between them. "So I'm wondering if you grew up watching *Elf* like I did."

"'We elves try to stick to the four main food groups,'" he quoted from the movie, "'candy, candy canes, candy corns, and syrup.'"

"I knew it!" She picked up the remote control and woke her TV. "I thought we could watch that tonight, but I'm open to other suggestions if you're opposed."

"I'm not opposed."

She paused the opening credits, rested the remote in her lap, and focused on him. "Hopefully Molly will be thoughtful enough to find a movie that you can both relate to and enjoy. But if she asks you to watch a movie with her that you're really not interested in at all, what should you say?"

He groaned. "Is this a trick question? You might want me to take one for the team and agree to watch her movie. Or you might want me to be brutally honest."

"Take your best guess, person who is smart enough to be serving food at the live nativity."

"What I would actually do in that situation is agree to watch the movie she picked." He shrugged. "I'm not that hard to please when it comes to movies. I can probably find something to like about her choice."

She nodded. "That's the answer I was going for. Right when you first start dating is the time to be agreeable and open minded. There'll be plenty of time for being disagreeable and closed minded once you've been dating for a year and a half or more."

He laughed.

She ate a bite of popcorn, smiling with her lips closed as she chewed.

"About Molly," he said. "I've decided to ask her out the night of the live nativity."

Her posture snapped straight. "She's going to be at the live nativity?"

"I have reason to think that she will be, yes. Do you have any recommendations for me?"

She toyed with the heart-shaped charm. "How about you tell me what you think might work best and then I'll provide feedback?"

He extended his arm across the sofa's back, which brought his fingers very near her hair. "I was thinking I'd wait for a time when things aren't busy. I can't ask her out while I'm shoveling cider into the hands of people waiting in a long line."

"True. I'm sure there will be plenty of volunteers present. So, when Molly's there, it shouldn't be a problem for you to step away for a few minutes and let someone else take up your duties."

"I plan to ask her how she's liking the nativity and then maybe ask her about her Christmas plans."

"Good and good." She tilted her head. "You might want to bring her some of the hot cider. It's forecasted to be a pretty chilly night. Oh! And if she looks cold, you could always ask if she's cold. If she says she is, then you could shrug out of your coat and offer it to her. Very gallant move. Just be sure to dress in layers so that you're not then standing there, teeth chattering."

"Noted," he said, though he wasn't confident in his ability to differentiate between whether she looked cold or didn't look cold.

"And then what are you going to say?" she asked.

"If she tells me that she's around for at least part of the holiday, I'll say something along the lines of, 'If you have time, maybe you and I can go to . . .'"

"To?"

"I'm not sure."

"Well, I'd avoid asking her to something on New Year's Eve. It's likely she already has plans with friends or family." She snapped her fingers. "What about the Winter Market and carnival that the Friends of the Hospital puts on? They have booths, sledding, rides, food. It's a lot of fun."

"Perfect," he said, amused. She hadn't been able to sit back and simply give him feedback on his ideas. It was in her nature to offer suggestions.

"Is that it?" she asked. "Anything else you have in mind?"

"No, that's all I've got. I'm sort of counting on the setting to help me out. Farm, nature, stars." He frowned. "Should I have something else in mind? Is that too simple?"

She considered the question. "I'm a fan of grand gestures in rom coms and in real-life situations when you're sure where the other person stands. But since you're unsure about Molly, I don't think it's a good idea for a horse-drawn carriage to come jangling up. Or for you to tell her you've hidden a note for her in baby Jesus's swaddling."

Baby Jesus's swaddling?

"Simple is the way to go," she said.

"That's a relief."

"Your plan's solid." She sang, "'Follow every

117

rainbow, until you find your dream,'" from *The Sound of Music.*

"Okay."

"I hope she says yes."

"I hope so too." Their eyes held.

She cleared her throat and put a few more inches of space between them. "I don't think you need any more of my help, Connor. Not as a dating consultant, anyway. I will, of course, be available at all times to name paintings and give your mom an excuse to eat whatever food she's craving."

"Thank you, for everything," he said, meaning it.

"As I told you at the start, you were already a diamond." The air between them thickened. "It's been fun, but I really didn't do very much. Turns out it's easy to shine a diamond."

Were her eyes wet? "I . . ." He didn't know what to say, other than maybe, *Shay, you're the diamond.*

"Movie?" she asked.

"Movie," he said, and she hit Play.

● ● ●

Two nights later, Connor returned to the house from his studio and overheard his mom on the phone.

"I have so much to be thankful for, Patsy," she was saying to the sister just a year and a half behind her in age. "So much."

He paused in the hallway. By the direction of the sound, he could tell Mom was sitting in her favorite living room chair.

"The only thing that would further ease my mind before I go is to see Connor . . . settled."

He winced.

Quiet. No doubt, she was listening to Patsy's reply.

"Yes," Mom said, "but she's as independent as they come. Her job's the most important thing to her and she'll likely be very happy going through life without a significant other." She had to be referring to his younger sister. "I'm fine with that. For her. Not for Connor."

Another stretch of silence.

Connor walked into the living room. Sure enough, she sat on the expected chair. Behind her, the Christmas lights he'd mounted on the edge of the roof weeks ago cast a glow against their dark front yard.

She eyeballed him and he gave her a look like, *You're busted.*

Her face turned instantly guilty. "Patsy? I'll

have to call you back."

Murmurs from the phone, then Mom disconnected and set the phone facedown on the arm of her chair. "Well?" she said defensively. "I *would* like to see you settled."

"I'm as independent as my sisters."

"Of course you are, but you're also a different case."

"Because?"

"Because you're in love with Shay."

He froze.

She regarded him with compassion. "I may have ALS but I'm still as observant as ever. You've always loved Shay."

His thoughts reeled. All his life his mom had shown him that she understood the things he never said and even tried to hide. Yet, every time, it surprised him.

He nodded because, yes. He loved Shay.

"When are you going to tell her?" she asked.

"Tomorrow."

Her face brightened. "Really?"

"Yes. But she might not be interested in me."

She outstretched her hand. He took hold, gripping firmly. Their journey together over the past two years raced through his memory. All the appointments, medicines, therapies. "If she's not interested in you," she said, "she's crazy."

"She's not crazy."

"Then she'll be interested in you."

"I don't want you to hang your sense of peace on my dating life."

"Okay, okay. I hear you. It's just . . . I love you."

"I love you, too."

"You've made me very proud of the son I raised. I don't want much . . . other than a cheeseburger," she added dryly. "But I *do* want you to be happy."

"I am happy."

"You could be happier," she said. "God is good. His plan is best. But I don't mind telling you, I'm going to pray tonight—and pray hard—that Shay sees in you what I see."

• • •

Low-level anxiety had been circling within Connor all day. The nativity was scheduled to start in thirty minutes, and the anxiety was still there.

Everything outdoors was ready, so the volunteers had gathered in the barn at Sugar Maple Farm, which Sam had cleared out in preparation for tonight. When the time came, they'd all move to their places outside. At the moment, a few of the character actors were still putting on the last pieces of their costumes and receiving hair or makeup touch-ups. The rest of them were standing around, talking.

Shay sat in a folding chair on the far side of the barn, as one of the volunteer stylists from the salon added waves to her hair. Connor pulled his attention from her, letting it rove over the space full of people, animals, and activity. In the corner, a gray donkey that looked much too old to carry a pregnant woman from Nazareth to Bethlehem blinked sleepily in its enclosure. The alpaca stared at the donkey nervously. The miniature cow appeared bored.

A group of shepherds discussed their golf swings. Two women with clipboards trailed his mother—who glowed tonight—as she leaned on her cane to slowly make her rounds. The older couple who'd brought the sheep to the site stood in front of the snack table, deciding between chips, pretzels, and Goldfish.

Leah, who'd dressed as one of the kings, stood next to Connor. As did Leah's boyfriend, Dr. Sebastian Grant, also dressed as a king.

Sebastian was one of the best heart surgeons in the country. A former foster kid, he'd climbed the ranks through sheer determination. Because

Connor and Sebastian had Ben as a mutual friend, Connor had interacted with Sebastian a few times in the past. His initial impression of Sebastian? That he was incredibly confident and intelligent, but also closed-off. Despite trying, Connor hadn't been able to connect with him at all.

However, Leah seemed to have transformed the blunt, unapologetic doctor. Sebastian couldn't take his eyes off his girlfriend. He smiled at her easily and there was almost always a physical link between them. Either her hand rested on his forearm, or their fingers interlaced, or he was freeing a piece of hair from her eyelashes, or she was whispering something in his ear.

No wonder Ben had stepped aside to make a way for these two. Clearly, they were a perfect match.

Ben and his family had other plans tonight, so he wouldn't be present. But Shay would be pleased because three of the Miracle Five *were* here. In addition to Sebastian, Natasha was present. She was playing the part of a shepherd. Even now, he heard her interrupt the talk about golf swings to explain how she was finishing up a year of living C.S. Lewisly. Strangely, she was also wearing terribly knitted mittens, which one of the costumers would definitely swap out for a style of gloves they'd approved.

Genevieve was also present, not surprising seeing as how she lived in the cottage on this property and was engaged to be married to the farm's owner, Sam.

"The crown suits you," Sebastian said to Leah. "Don't you agree Connor?"

"I do."

"It doesn't suit me," Sebastian stated, looking toward his forehead, where a huge fake gold crown rested on his dark hair.

Leah rolled her eyes. "No one's buying your false humility, darling."

"Did it ring false?" Sebastian asked.

"Humility from doctors always rings false," she teased. "Connor and I and the rest of the people in America know how arrogant you all are."

"Want to know something that I'm very arrogant about?"

"Inspiring the crushes of young female nurses and saving the lives of infants?"

"The fact that I won you over," he said smugly. "In fact, I think I should announce to all these people how proud I am of that." He straightened, cupped a hand around his mouth, and angled toward the center of the barn.

Laughing, Leah clapped her palm over his

mouth. "The fact that you've already arrogantly announced to Connor and me how proud you are of that will suffice."

"I'm not sure that it will."

"It will." She drew Sebastian's hand down and linked their pinky fingers. "Right, Connor?"

"Right." His only contribution to this conversation seemed to be serving as a yes-man for their banter.

Genevieve approached. She was portraying Mary tonight, and they'd dressed her in pale blue robes. An even paler blue piece of fabric draped over her head, framing her pretty face and the long hair falling forward over her shoulders. All six of the sheep trailed behind her like lovestruck puppies. "I don't have any idea why these sheep keep following me everywhere I go," Genevieve said to them. "I think they're confused. I'm not a shepherd."

"Are you Little Bo Peep?" Sebastian asked.

"A sheep whisperer?" Connor suggested.

"As you both know, I'm a Bible study author and teacher."

"Maybe that's what they're picking up on," Leah said. "The biblical link between them and you."

"The Bible talks a lot about sheep," Connor

pointed out helpfully.

"Feed my sheep," Sebastian quoted.

"My sheep listen to my voice," Leah added.

"Take care of my sheep," Connor said.

One of the sheep casually gummed the fold of Genevieve's robe.

Sam joined them, dressed as Joseph in brown robes. He was one of the few lucky men in the room who hadn't been forced to wear a headpiece. "Are these sheep following you around like I do?" he asked Genevieve.

"Yes. Could it be that they're attracted to the smell of my perfume?"

"If so, they have good taste. I'm attracted to the smell of your perfume."

Genevieve smiled up at Sam, seeming to get distracted.

"What?" Sam asked.

"You look great," she told him.

"Seriously?" Sam looked down at himself, then back at her.

"Let's just say, if I was Mary, I'd be delighted if you were my betrothed."

"Well. I am your betrothed."

"And I'm delighted." Sheep stood at attention on both sides of her, like trained Dobermans.

"You're not going to become pregnant with

God's baby, are you?" Sam asked her.

"If I become pregnant after our wedding day, the father is going to be considerably more human," she shot back.

"Genevieve," Sebastian asked, "can you make some Manchego cheese out of sheep's milk for me?"

"Baaa," the sheep on her right said.

"I could use a wool sweater," Connor said.

"I like to eat mutton," Sam commented.

"*Gentlemen*," Genevieve said. "I don't believe Mary had time to give her attention to Manchego, wool sweaters, and mutton on the night of Jesus's birth."

They continued their joking conversation as Connor's vision strayed back to Shay.

The live nativity had new donors this year, so their angel costumes had been upgraded. Instead of wearing choir-robe-type clothing, all the angels were dressed in what looked like floor-length coats with pretend fur around the high collars. The colors of the coats ranged from light beige to bright white. Shay's coat was in the middle of that spectrum, a deep ivory color.

He'd been trying to meet Shay's eye since he'd entered the barn. Unlike at the ugly sweater party, he wasn't having success. She seemed subdued tonight. A little down, maybe?

His mom walked over to her, and Shay rose to hug her. She settled back into the chair so the stylist could finish. Then Mom and Shay talked easily.

Watching them, the nervousness he'd been battling slowly melted away. By degrees, certainty took its place.

He wasn't sure of how Shay would respond to him tonight. But he was sure of the most important things.

He was sure of her.

He was sure that no one could love her like he could.

Chapter Eight

When Penny had initially asked Shay to portray an angel in the live nativity, she'd agreed purely to make Penny happy. She hadn't expected to get anything out of it.

But once the nativity was underway, something sort of . . . miraculous had begun to happen. She'd become very still, and the stillness had given her other senses a chance to expand. She'd looked, really looked, deeply at the stars and the slips of cloud skating across them. She'd listened to one beautiful, historic carol after another. She'd smelled woodsmoke from a distant chimney and caught occasional snatches of the cinnamon perfume favored by the angel standing next to her.

As Penny had indicated, the angels were positioned back and to the side of the manger scene. Their group had been very cleverly lit, so that their skin shimmered thanks to the highlighter the makeup artist had applied.

A few of the shepherds were stationed before them, sometimes kneeling, sometimes sitting, depending on what was most comfortable for their knees and backs at any given time.

Someone had built a frame for the manger scene from planks of wood. The planks rose up on either side of Mary and Joseph and formed a point above them, where a lit star gleamed. Straw drifted over the sides of an authentic-looking manger. Instead of a real baby or a doll as a stand-in for Jesus, they'd placed a light at the base of the manger, which sent warm rays upward. The light created a halo, bathing the people that surrounded it.

The incredible beauty of Mary and Joseph flanking the glowing manger struck Shay forcefully.

Yes, it was outwardly charming. Three of the five Miracle Five were taking part, which was jaw-dropping. Mary and Joseph, clearly in love, made a striking couple. The shepherds held staffs in their hands. The kings wore lavish robes. The sweet-faced donkey swished its tail. The cow was so bizarrely small it looked fake. The sheep seemed obsessed with Genevieve, and one had even rested its chin on Genevieve's lap.

This nativity was about much more than outward charm, though. Seeing how real and living the participants were reminded her how real and living the participants in that first Christmas had been. All of them, people just like these, prone to mistakes, heartaches, joys. They'd been going about their ordinary lives when this wildly extraordinary thing had occurred. They'd experienced the birth of a baby who was completely divine, yet also as completely human as they were.

As she was.

The melancholy that had occasionally dragged at her this December had been silenced by the thing that was truest, most lovely, and most powerful about Christmas . . .

Its actual meaning. Jesus.

Who'd grown up and sacrificed Himself to save the world.

Grateful tears had stung her eyes several times and she'd spent much of the evening praying.

As if by unspoken agreement, the hundreds of people who'd come to view the nativity had responded with quiet reverence. From her vantage point, she'd seen on their faces that many were feeling what she was feeling.

One older man had stood at the fringes for a full hour, tears trickling down his face. Children gazed at the scene with open mouths. Busy adults paused, the stress easing from their posture. The only person who hadn't responded with proper respect was Gabe. When he'd stopped by, he'd pulled funny face after funny face, in an effort to make her break character and laugh. She'd resisted until he'd started moving his lanky body in geeky dance moves. With supreme self-control, she'd avoided inappropriate church giggles in favor of a smile. Surreptitiously, she shot him angelic jazz hands.

She'd been to the nativity as an observer a couple of times in the past, long ago. It hadn't impacted her deeply on those occasions.

But this time it had. In just a few hours' time, Shay had become a fervent supporter of Misty River's live nativity. She'd dress in costume until she was a very old angel, indeed. Or she'd help in other ways to ensure that Connor's mom's project of the heart continued.

By rights, the transcendent experience she'd been having should have protected her from thoughts of Connor and Molly. If only it had. She'd been unable to stop herself from keeping an eye on Connor and trying to figure out Molly's identity. Still no success at that.

Was there any chance that Molly was her? She'd thought for a split second that maybe there was a chance when he'd brought a plant to dinner the other night. But he'd had lots of opportunities that night to tell her if she was Molly. And he hadn't taken any of them.

So, stop getting your hopes up, Shay. This was a case of wanting something badly enough that you're imagining it into existence. He probably asked Molly out tonight and she probably said yes and you're definitely going to act happy for them.

The choir performed its final song. Then Penny thanked the community members, the choir, the cast. As Penny closed in prayer, Shay's gratitude mingled with a dash of disappointment. The most wonderful evening she'd had in a long time was coming to an end.

"We praise the one who sent His son," Penny prayed. "The true source of hope. The true source of love. The true source of peace. The true source of life. Merry Christmas. Amen."

"Amen," the crowd responded.

The choir burst into a few famous bars of the "Hallelujah Chorus." "'And He shall reign forever and ever!'" they sang.

When they finished on the last triumphant note, everyone clapped enthusiastically. It was only then, when people drifted toward their cars or toward the barn to take off their costumes, that the volume of conversation rose. Shay and her fellow angels chatted warmly for a few minutes, then dispersed.

She looked up, taking one minute longer to seal this night into her memory. On a sigh, she headed in the direction of the barn, a few hundred yards away.

As she walked, the hem of her coat thumped against the front of her ankles. She caught sight of Connor cutting toward her from where he'd been working serving cider.

Tenderness welled high and fast.

He'd been humble enough to ask for her help and good-natured enough to take her advice. He looked gorgeous this evening in her favorite "artist in residence" outfit from their shopping trip. Cardigan. Blazer. His hands were sunk in the blazer's pockets and his cheeks were doing that hot rugby player thing again.

They came to a stop facing one another. An angel and a handsome, wildly talented, auburn-haired man.

"Good evening," he said. She loved his perceptive gray eyes. The lips that tilted up at the very edges. His was a thoughtful face, the face of a man who was observant, who took time to care about people.

He'd been a thoughtful kid, she remembered. But that characteristic had only increased over time.

A pang of yearning so real it felt like a hunger pang struck her.

"Good evening," she replied.

"How was the nativity for you?"

"Incredible, actually. I was—am . . . sort of awestruck by it. Not just *it*—the scene we helped portray tonight—but by the actual thing tonight represented. My mind is blown right now."

"I know what you mean. It has that effect on a lot of people, which is why Mom champions it every year."

"I intend to champion it right alongside her from now on."

"Me too." They shared a smile and a beat of mutual understanding. "What are your plans for the next few days?"

"I'll be spending most of tomorrow with my brother and his wife, which will be fabulous. Then I'll be spending the rest of Christmas Eve and Christmas day with my mom or dad, which won't be as fabulous. But will be better than usual, I think, after this. I feel like I've had my perspective recalibrated." She straightened the tall neck of her coat. "What are you going to be up to?"

"All of our usual family traditions. A lot of noise. Some arguing between my sisters, my brother-in-law, and my sister's kids. So much food we'll be stuffed. Too many presents."

"So, in other words, it'll be pretty great?"

"Yeah."

"I'm glad."

He looked away for a moment, then back at her. "If you have time over the break, would you like to go with me to the Winter Market and carnival?"

Hmm? She wrinkled her forehead, trying to understand. "Connor, your training's done. The diamond is shining. You don't need any more practice."

"I'm not asking if you'll go with me because I need practice." He spoke calmly, then studied her expectantly. "It's you, Shay. I've been in love with you since we were kids."

Her bottom lip sagged downward, and it was like the choir had struck up the "Hallelujah Chorus" all over again. This time, though, just in her head.

"You're Molly," he said.

She lifted her hands to her cheeks. "I am?"

He nodded, smiling. "It's always been you. For me. For years I thought I'd outgrow my feelings for you, but I never did. They'll outlast me, I'm sure of it. I love your personality. How daring you are. How honest. I even love your pink tennis shoes. And I really love when you sing lyrics of Broadway songs."

What!

Her brain cartwheeled back through the things he'd said about Molly. He'd said he'd been attracted to her confidence in herself. He'd said he'd been too shy to ask her out and then circumstances had stopped him. When she'd asked him how much he liked Molly, he'd pointed to a masterpiece of a painting motivated by love.

Oh. My. Goodness. Her hands slid together under her chin, knotting.

"I would have brought you some cider," he continued, "but we ran out. And I would have asked if you're cold, but as far as I can tell, you don't look cold. So I didn't ask."

She laughed with joy and astonishment. "I'm definitely not cold." In fact, heat was rushing up her like tide onto a beach. "I'm Molly?"

"You're Molly." He grinned.

She'd been jealous of herself. All along, she was Molly. "Is . . . is a horse and carriage going to come jangling up?"

He hitched a shoulder. "I wasn't opposed to a

horse and carriage, but apparently, grand gestures are only good in rom coms and situations when you know how the other person feels about you. I don't. Know how you feel about me."

She was having trouble finding her breath. Maybe because her heart was thumping so fast. She extended a palm, facing it toward him as if she was setting it against a pane of glass. He carefully placed his palm against hers, his artist's fingers longer than hers. Wonder zinged from the contact. Their hands interlaced. He bent his arm and set their joined hands against his chest, bringing her close to him.

"No woman has ever compared to you in my mind," he said.

"You cut your hair," she whispered, "and shaved your beard and bought new clothes and ice skated . . . for me?"

"For you," he confirmed. "I wanted to learn how to become someone you'd consider. And I wanted to spend time with you." Sheepishly, he scratched the side of his jaw with his free hand. "It was a risky plan and I'm sorry I misled you, but it was all I could think of. I'd ice skate every day for you, if that's what you wanted."

"That won't be necessary."

"I'm crazy about you."

"I didn't know."

"I always have been. Crazy about you."

Silence passed between them like a caress. She was overwhelmed in the best way—trying to process . . . This was happening! To her. Connor liked *her*! He'd done all this for her. "I'm pleased to inform you that your dating consultant is crazy about you, too."

He looked afraid to believe her.

"I am definitely, certifiably crazy about you," she said. "And I would definitely, certifiably love to go to the Winter Market with you."

"Shay." The single syllable held deep emotion. He said no more and if she had to guess, she'd say that was because amazement had stolen additional words.

She knew the feeling.

"I'm only sorry," she said, "that I didn't realize how you felt about me and how I felt about you sooner."

"Looking back, I think there was a reason for that. It wasn't the right time."

"We were too young," she acknowledged. "But now? Now feels *so* right."

"Exactly right."

He kissed her and she kissed him back in a field dotted with people, a stable, a shining star, and sheep trailing behind Genevieve.

The kiss went from soft to passionate back to soft again, so good it literally made her weak in her long-underwear-clad knees.

When she came up for air, her lips tingled as they observed each other. Over his shoulder, quite a distance away, Shay spotted movement and realized it was Penny, pumping her raised fists in the air.

"Merry Christmas," he said.

"Merry Christmas."

She'd wondered what it would feel like to have a boyfriend who was willing to go the extra mile.

It felt like a sacred trust, like hope, and amazing good fortune she didn't deserve.

Come to think of it . . .

It felt a lot like Christmas.

"I have loved you with an everlasting love."
Jeremiah 31:3

Read Luke Dempsey's love story!

Turn to Me

Guilt has defined Luke Dempsey's life. But it was self-destructiveness that landed him in prison. When his friend and fellow inmate lays dying shortly before Luke's release, the older man reveals he's left a string of clues for his daughter Finley that will lead her to the treasure he's hidden. Worried that she won't be the only one pursuing the treasure, he begs Luke to protect her, and Luke promises he will.

Finley Sutherland, owner of an animal rescue center and dogged defender of lost causes, accepts Luke's help with the treasure hunt while secretly planning to help him in return—by coaxing him to embrace the forgiveness he's long denied himself.

As they draw closer to the mysterious cache, their reasons for resisting one another begin to crumble and Luke realizes his promise will be harder to keep than he'd anticipated. He'll do his best to shield Finley from unseen threats. But who's going to shield him from losing his heart?

Romances by Becky Wade

MISTY RIVER ROMANCE
Take a Chance on Me (#0.5)
Stay with Me (#1)
Let It Be Me (#2)
You and Me (#2.5)
Turn to Me (#3)

BRADFORD SISTERS ROMANCE
Then Came You (#0.5)
True to You (#1)
Falling for You (#2)
Because of You (#2.5)
Sweet on You (#3)

THE PORTER FAMILY
Undeniably Yours (#1)
Meant to Be Mine (#2)
A Love Like Ours (#3)
The Proposal (#3.5)
Her One and Only (#4)

Stand-alone Romances
My Stubborn Heart
Love in the Details

Sign up for Becky's E-Newsletter

For the latest news about Becky's upcoming books, exclusive giveaways, and more, subscribe to Becky's free quarterly e-newsletter at www.beckywade.com

About the Author

Becky Wade's a California native who attended Baylor University, met and married a Texan, and settled in Dallas. She published historical romances for the general market before putting her career on hold for several years to care for her three children. When God called her back to writing, Becky knew He meant for her to turn her attention to Christian fiction. She loves writing emotional, modern, and inspirational contemporary romance! She's the Christy and Carol Award–winning author of *My Stubborn Heart*, the PORTER FAMILY series, the BRADFORD SISTERS ROMANCE series, and the MISTY RIVER ROMANCE series. To learn more about Becky and her books, visit her website at www.beckywade.com.

Connect with Becky

You'll find Becky on Facebook as Author Becky Wade and on Instagram, Twitter, and Pinterest as BeckyWadeWriter.

Made in the USA
Las Vegas, NV
11 November 2021

34216642R00090